# He came to her in the night.

Taylor knew it was Mark trying to influence her thoughts. Eight years had passed since he'd stirred her to dark, sensual passion, since he'd used his hands and teeth and tongue to bring her to writhing, mindless ecstasy.

Those years could well have been mere weeks. Days. She could feel his presence in her hotel room. The impression was so real, so vivid, he might have been looming over her bed.

"No! You're not getting into my head."

Yanking the sheet to her chin, Taylor stubbornly refused to acknowledge the sensations crawling over her skin.

"Forget it. I'm not letting you in," Taylor said aloud. "Don't think about the past. Focus on the mission."

Despite her fierce attempt to control her thoughts, a subtle semiawareness shimmered just below the level of consciousness.

"I won't do this! Do you hear me, Wolfson? I refuse to do this!"

The sensations continued to creep over her. Slow. Dark. Insidious. Stirring her blood.

## *MERLINE LOVELACE*

A former Air Force officer, Merline Lovelace served tours at the Pentagon and at bases all around the world. When she hung up her uniform for the last time, she decided to try her hand at writing. She now has more than seventy novels published in twenty-eight languages.

When not glued to her keyboard, working on a book, Merline and her own handsome hero enjoy golf and traveling to exotic spots all over the world. Check out her Web site at www.merlinelovelace.com for pictures of her travels and information about her upcoming releases.

# MERLINE LOVELACE
## MIND GAMES

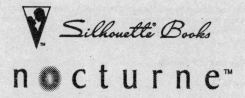

Silhouette Books

nocturne™

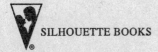 SILHOUETTE BOOKS

ISBN-13: 978-0-373-61784-5
ISBN-10:    0-373-61784-4

MIND GAMES

Copyright © 2008 by Merline Lovelace

This edition published by arrangement with Harlequin Books S.A.

www.silhouettenocturne.com

**Printed in U.S.A.**

Dear Reader,

Years ago, while I was serving as operations officer for a Special Ops training unit, one of my duties was to authorize requisitions for live goats. I didn't ask (and didn't really want to know!) where those goats eventually wound up.

Recently I stumbled across a book with the intriguing title *Men Who Stare at Goats,* by Jon Ronson. Of course I had to pick it up and read it. The book describes a supersecret Army program in the late '70s that was created to harness the power of mind over matter and use that power to influence other living creatures.

So when I decided to write a novel for Silhouette's wonderful Nocturne line, I immediately focused on the subject of mental telepathy. Also known as psychokinesis, or remote influencing, the subject remains one of intense scientific study today at prestigious universities and research institutes around the world.

I hope you enjoy my foray into the world of paranormal ops—and into the even more mysterious and powerful force that is known as love.

Merline Lovelace

For my one, my only, my Al,
who holds my heart and mind forever

# *Chapter 1*

USAF Captain Taylor Chase slowed her rental car to a crawl and squinted through the deepening September dusk. She'd plotted her route using the latest satellite imagery. With its incredible detail, the digital map showed every feature of the surrounding countryside, from the round silo she'd passed two miles back to this stand of tall, primeval pines that seemed to have swallowed her whole. Now all she had to find was the turnoff leading to the Wolf's lair.

Amazing, she thought as she steered through

the spiky shadows thrown by the pines. Here she was, smack in the middle of New Jersey. New Jersey, for God's sake! The Garden State. The truck-farm capital of the world. She had expected the rolling farmlands she'd driven through after leaving the Turnpike at the Princeton exit. The university town looked pretty much as she'd anticipated, too. And damned if ivy didn't actually cover the walls of the centuries-old center of learning that dominated the historic town.

But this… This lonely stretch of road lined with silent, brooding pines made Taylor feel as though she were driving through a Transylvanian forest instead of rural America.

She supposed she shouldn't be surprised that her target had chosen this isolated spot to go to ground. The extensive dossier Pentagon analysts had compiled on Dr. Mark Wolfson only confirmed what Taylor already knew from personal experience. The zoologist was brilliant and sexy as all hell, but preferred the company of lab rats to humans.

With one notable exception. Grimacing at the memory of their brief, disastrous affair, Taylor switched on the car's headlights. White arcs sliced through the now-purple dusk. As the rental crawled along the two-lane road, she reviewed her strategy.

She'd opted not to call for an appointment with Wolfson at his Princeton University research center. She suspected he would flatly refuse to see her. More to the point, what she had to say to him was better said in private, away from curious lab techs or research assistants. Surprise, Taylor had decided, was the best tactic when confronting a man you'd once told to take his laboratory full of test equipment and shove it where the sun doesn't shine.

Hunching over the wheel, she peered through the gloom. Was that a turnoff? It was.

"Finally!"

Ignoring the prominently posted Private Property, No Trespassing signs, she nosed onto the unpaved road. With each turn of the wheels, the broad-needle pines seemed to close in. Darkness, thick and black and unrelenting, now enveloped her. The sharp tang of resin spiked the night air coming in through the vents.

When the scent of wood smoke pierced even that heavy tang, Taylor knew she'd tracked the Wolf to his lair. Moments later she spotted the glow of illuminated windows staring at her like unblinking owls' eyes. Shoving the car into Park, she cut the engine and climbed out.

She stood for a moment, listening to the breeze that sighed through the pines. Reviewing her strategy. Remembering her last session with Mark Wolfson.

Her belly tightened. The tips of her breasts tingled. A tremor of dark, seductive pleasure shivered down her spine. As if it was yesterday, she heard the rasp in his deep voice when he'd whispered that her wild passion exceeded even his most optimistic calculations.

The physical sensations gripping Taylor were so strong, so intense, they almost obliterated the memory of her fury when his words finally penetrated her postcoital haze.

She'd been an experiment. Nothing more. A step up from the rats he usually worked with, granted. But an experiment nonetheless.

A sharp sting jerked Taylor from the past. She looked down, saw she'd dug her nails deep into her palms. Disgusted, she unclenched her fists and shoved the memories out of her head.

All that happened a long time ago. Almost

eight years. She'd put the humiliating episode behind her. She hoped to God Mark Wolfson had done the same.

He'd better have, she thought grimly. The success of her mission depended on her ability to convince Wolfson to accompany her to a heavily guarded private island in the Caribbean.

"Okay, Chase," she told herself sternly, starting for the house. "It's showtime."

The low growl was her only warning.

It came at her from the trees off to her left. The hairs on the back of her neck lifting, Taylor reached instinctively for the weapon tucked inside her purse and spun around. She heard a branch snap. Saw a dark blur. Had less than a heartbeat to react before that blur took on the shape of a racing dog.

Not just a dog, she realized as her heart jumped into her throat. An attack dog. Big and fast and shaggy, leaping right at her.

"Down! Sit! Shit!"

Her fingers locked around the butt of her Glock but she didn't have time to whip it out. Fangs bared, eyes narrowed to slits, the animal went for her throat.

Taylor flung up her other arm. Her one hope, her only hope, was to put every ounce of her strength into a swing and bat the beast aside. She thrust back a foot to brace herself, felt her heel give, and went down.

She hit hard. The back of her head whacked the ground. The arm she'd flung up crumpled, leaving her defenseless.

The last thing she saw were glistening, salivating fangs.


Taylor Chase.

Christ!

His jaw tight, Mark curled his fingers in the ruff of the animal hunkered beside him. Emotions he'd thought long dead stormed through him as he studied the unconscious woman he'd carried into the house.

He hadn't recognized her at first. Her face was thinner than in her college days and she'd cut off the careless tumble of curls that used to spill over her shoulders. She now wore her dark mahogany hair in a short, shining cap instead of the silky mane that had trailed across his pillow.

His hands clenched in the shaggy ruff. The dog at his side lifted his head in question.

*Sorry, Tikal.*

Smoothing the animal's fur, Mark continued his inventory. The full, sensual mouth was the same. So was the chin she could set at such a stubborn angle. Of all the graduate assistants assigned to the zoology department at the University of Michigan, Taylor Chase had given him the most grief…literally and figuratively.

She'd also given him the most intense pleasure he'd ever experienced, before or since.

Before he could block them, the images jumped into Mark's head. Taylor laughing at some inane joke made by one of the other assistants. Frowning as she tried to interpret test results. Grinning wickedly as she unbuttoned her lab coat to reveal nothing but smooth, sleek skin.

Sweat popped out on Mark's brow. Swearing viciously, he reminded himself this woman had put him through hell. He'd returned the favor, he recalled with brutal honesty. The difference was, he hadn't intended to.

So what was she doing here? Why had she tracked him down after all these years?

He glanced at the shoulder bag he'd retrieved after carrying her inside. The blue steel automatic in her purse gave the questions swirling around in

Mark's head a sharp, serrated edge. That, and the leather case containing a shield and an ID that identified Taylor Rebecca Chase as an agent with the USAF Office of Special Investigations.

A low moan brought his gaze whipping back to the woman stretched out on the leather cushions. The creature beside him tensed.

*She's friend, Tikal. Not foe. I think.*

The qualified endorsement confused the animal. His ears went back. A rumble rose from deep in his throat.

The growl appeared to penetrate Taylor's daze. Her brow creased. Her lids fluttered. With a sound that was closer to a grunt than a groan, she opened her eyes.

Confusion blanked their emerald depths for a moment or two. When they fixed on Mark, disgust and distrust swept through them in equal parts. Then her gaze dropped to the creature at his side. To her credit, she didn't so much as flinch.

Green eyes locked with blue. Woman and dog measured each other warily. After a short staring contest, Taylor met Mark's gaze once more.

"That's quite a welcome you give visitors, Wolfson."

"Only those who arrive unannounced and un-invited. What are you doing here?"

"I want to talk to you."

"We said all we needed to say to each other eight years ago."

With an impatient frown, she started to sit up. A warning growl from Tikal kept her pinned to the leather cushions.

"Call off your watchdog."

"Not until you tell me why you're here."

Her mouth twisted sardonically. "Is the big bad wolf afraid of little me?"

"I'd say I had good reason to be, wouldn't you?"

A swift retort rose to Taylor's lips. With some effort, she bit it back. The anger and hurt had been mutual, although she had to admit Mark had taken the brunt of the blame after word leaked that he'd not only had an affair with a grad student, but he'd also experimented on her without her knowledge or consent.

He'd denied it, of course. When hauled in front of the University of Michigan's Faculty Review Committee, Dr. Wolfson swore he'd confined his experiments to laboratory animals and had never attempted to remotely influence the behavior of any human, Taylor Chase included.

The Committee had determined there was insufficient evidence to substantiate the charge of improper experimentation, but had censured the professor for tumbling into bed with a student. They'd also imposed such restrictions on his research that Mark had eventually resigned in disgust.

His reputation in the areas of psychic research and remote influencing was so well established by then, however, that a dozen other universities had courted him with offers of fat grants and dedicated research facilities.

Taylor wasn't surprised he'd ended up at Princeton. The university had been one of the first in the nation to establish an institute devoted to the scientific study of consciousness-related psychic phenomena. The institute's interdisciplinary staff of engineers, physicists, psychologists, behaviorists and humanists included some of the greatest minds in the country, probably the world. Mark Wolfson certainly fell into that category.

Looking at him now, Taylor found little trace of the slightly nerdy, if undeniably sexy, prof she'd teased and tormented. That Mark had been quiet, withdrawn, unsure how to respond to her flirting. At first.

She could still remember how his blue eyes had blinked owlishly behind his glasses the first day she'd swept into his lab and announced she'd applied for his vacant assistantship. Despite his six-two frame and the impressive set of shoulders covered by his lab coat, he'd appeared more than a little overwhelmed by her breezy self-assurance.

This Mark appeared anything but. He still sported those broad shoulders, now covered in a denim shirt with the sleeves rolled up. The glasses were gone, though, making his eyes appear a deeper, more intense blue above the five-o'clock shadow darkening his cheeks and chin. Taylor suspected she'd contributed to the strands of silver threading through his jet-black hair. He was wearing it longer these days. Almost as long and shaggy as the coat of the creature still watching her with a steady, unwinking stare.

The animal looked two-parts Husky, one part wild dog. Or wolf. His fur was mostly silver with streaks of gray and black, and his eyes were as blue and unfriendly as his master's. Irritated at being skewered by those twin hostile stares, Taylor made another attempt to sit up.

The dog reacted immediately. Rising up on its haunches, it issued a warning growl. His quivering black gums revealed the incisors Taylor suspected she'd see in her sleep for some time to come.

Ignoring the throbbing ache at the back of her skull, she emptied her mind and tried to focus her inner energy as Mark had taught her.

*Sit, fella. Sit. I'm just here to talk.*

Her attempt to influence another creature's behavior using only her mind didn't work. It never had, dammit.

Then again, if she'd acquired any of Dr. Mark Wolfson's unique skills, she wouldn't be here, determined to convince him to put his life on the line.

"Tell your pal to back off, Mark. What I need to talk to you about is urgent."

"Does it have anything to do with the badge and the automatic in your purse?"

Taylor's mouth tightened. She wasn't surprised he'd searched her bag. She would have done the same, given the circumstances. Still, it irritated her no end that she'd surrendered control of her

weapon to a civilian. Particularly this civilian.
That didn't bode well for her ability to convince
him she would provide the muscle if he provided
the brainpower for the dangerous mission ahead.

"Yes," she snapped, "it involves the badge and
the gun. Tell the dog to back off."

If she'd needed proof Mark was the right man
for the mission, he gave it now. Without so much
as a twitch of an eyelid, he projected a silent
signal.

The dog responded with a swish of its tail and
padded to a throw rug positioned in front of a
stone fireplace. Using its muzzle and forepaws, it
bunched the rug into a satisfactory pile and circled
a few times before settling.

Taylor let out the first full breath since she'd
come awake to the mother of all headaches and
two pairs of suspicious blue eyes. The throbbing
pain was subsiding. The wariness in Mark's face
wasn't.

Enough of the headache remained, however, to
make itself felt as Taylor shoved upright. Her
wince elicited a grudging offer.

"I think I've got some aspirin upstairs," Mark
said. "Wait here."

She used his brief absence to make a quick sweep of what she could see of his home. The dossier Intelligence had compiled indicated Wolfson had done most of the renovations to the centuries-old farmhouse himself.

The smoke-blackened ceiling beams looked original. So did the stone fireplace. The peg-and-plank flooring was new, Taylor guessed, as was the loft that almost doubled the living space.

The furniture had been designed more for comfort and utility than style. Both the man-size leather chair and the sofa she occupied showed signs of use. The coffee table was a solid block of polished granite, with books and journals littering every inch of its surface. More volumes were crammed into the built-in shelves that took up one whole wall.

Taylor itched to get a closer look at some of those volumes. Although she'd abandoned her graduate studies at the University of Michigan after the fiasco of her affair with Mark and joined the air force instead, she'd eventually completed her master's in behavioral science. Her chosen field of study had served her well during her five years as an air force undercover agent. God knew she'd gotten up close and personal with some really weird personality types.

Good thing none of the criminals she'd investigated had access to Dr. Mark Wolfson's research into the power of the mind over matter. Remote influencing could up the crime rate considerably. Taylor cringed at the thought of some creep silently signaling a kid to wander away from a school playground or convincing a prison guard to look the other way at the most opportune moment. *That* would have opened some real scary possibilities.

"Here. Take these."

Mark passed her two aspirin and a glass of water and folded his long frame into the overstuffed leather chair. His ice-blue eyes were no friendlier than when he'd departed the room a few moments ago.

"What's this about, Taylor?"

She downed the aspirin and plunged into the morass. "You've heard of Oscar Hayes?"

He flicked an impatient hand. "Of course, I have. We co-authored a paper on the genetic differences in the nesting behavior of leatherback turtles some years back. Our work diverged after I became more interested in remote influences on animal behavior and Hayes got heavily into research involving xeno-transplantation."

Xeno-transplantation. The science of genetically engineering living organisms for the purpose of harvesting their cells or organs and transplanting them into humans.

The controversial concept took cloning to the next level. In the process, it raised the hopes of millions of desperately ill patients around the world. It was also the reason Taylor had sought out the man she'd once vowed to cut off at the knees if their paths ever crossed again.

"Dr. Hayes walked away from his home and his work two months ago," she said grimly. "He's since surfaced on a private island in the Caribbean. We're not sure whether he was snatched or purposely went underground."

"We?"

"The FBI, the CIA, and the Air Force Office of Special Investigations. You saw my credentials when you rifled through my bag. I'm an agent with the OSI."

"Since when?"

"Since about a year after I dropped out of grad school."

She hadn't intended that as a dig. Whatever regret Taylor experienced after leaving the University of Michigan had long since dissipated. She loved what she now did.

Mark didn't know that, however. Guilt tinged with remorse flickered across his face. Good! Taylor wouldn't hesitate to play on both emotions if necessary.

"Why is the air force concerned with Dr. Hayes's disappearance?"

"He was working on a highly classified project for us. We know he's holed up on an island off the coast of St. Kitts, in the Eastern Caribbean. We *think* he's being held against his will. We also think an international consortium that specializes in selling organs on the black market intends to exploit his research."

Mark's low whistle woke the dog. Ears pricked forward, it raised its head and gave a little whine. Mark must have sent a silent assurance as it dropped its muzzle onto its paws and dozed off again.

"Let me get this straight."

Hunching forward, Taylor's former professor and lover drilled into her with his penetrating blue eyes.

"You think this rogue consortium intends to genetically engineer organs and pass them off as human on the black market?"

"We do."

"And you're not sure whether Hayes is in on the deal or not?"

"Correct."

"Then I repeat. Why do you need me?"

"You're my ticket onto the island. A stranger would be turned away, but Hayes knows you. We're betting he wouldn't turn his back on a colleague in distress."

Setting aside the water glass still clutched in her hand, Taylor outlined the plan she and her counterparts at the Pentagon had worked out.

"Here's the scenario. You've been working night and day and have finally decided to take a busman's holiday. You've rented a sloop to cruise the Caribbean to observe and document the effect of remote influencing on marine mammals. I've accompanied you."

"In what capacity?"

She'd stumbled over that during discussions at the Pentagon. The sloop would have to be small enough for a two-person crew to handle. That suggested an intimacy beyond mere professional association.

"I'm your navigator-slash-research assistant-slash-girlfriend." Ignoring the sudden tightening of his mouth, she continued. "Our boat will hit a reef just off the island. We'll radio distress signals, making sure we broadcast your name, and row ashore. Hayes will recognize you and, hopefully, convince his associates to let us into their facilities."

"And then?"

"Then," she replied with calculated nonchalance, "we assess the situation, extract the doc if necessary, and get the hell out of Dodge."

"No."

The flat negative left no room for negotiation. Taylor forged ahead anyway.

"No to which part of the plan? Capsizing the sloop? Rowing ashore? The girlfriend bit?"

"No to the whole deal."

She'd warned the folks at the Pentagon that Wolfson would take some convincing. She tried the calm, rational approach first.

"Look, Mark, I know we have a history. As a matter of fact, that's why the air force tapped me for this mission. When our people combed through Hayes's background, they saw you had coauthored that paper with him. They also made the link between you and me."

They could hardly miss it. Although university officials had managed to hush up the messy affair, Taylor underwent a detailed background investigation prior to acceptance into the Federal Law Enforcement Academy and the Air Force Office of Special Investigations. The OSI background checks included one-on-one interviews with DOD investigators. She'd cringed a little at having to admit her stupidity in allowing herself be used as a sexual guinea pig, but had made no attempt to cover up her reason for leaving grad school in mid-semester.

"If they uncovered a link between us," Mark countered, "they must know we severed it years ago."

"They do. That doesn't change the fact that I worked with you for the better part of a year. I'll have to get up to speed on your current research, but I'm confident I can play my role with…"

"Which role?" he interjected sardonically. "Navigator, research assistant or lover?"

Ice edged her smile. "As I was saying, I'll have to get up to speed on your current research. But I know my way around a behavioral science lab. I can still talk cognitive organization theory and neural dissonance with some credibility. Enough to get my foot in the door of the facilities on that island, anyway."

"If you can walk the walk and talk the talk, you don't need me."

"Hayes doesn't know me from squat. Your name will carry more weight with him and whoever's on that island."

His expression hard and unyielding, Mark shook his head. "You and I collaborated once before, with disastrous results. I'm not interested in a repeat performance." He pushed out of his chair and scooped up her purse. "I'll walk you to your car."

The dog scrabbled up as well, its claws clicking on the wooden floor. Man and beast regarded Taylor expectantly. She didn't budge.

"I mentioned that Hayes was working on a highly classified project for the air force. I can't go into the specifics, but I can tell you it involves genetically engineered skin for the treatment of seriously burned or wounded troops."

Like her brother. Two years younger than Taylor, Danny had opted for the marines instead of the air force. He'd been in Iraq less than a week when his HumVee hit an IED and exploded into a flaming fireball. Eighteen months later Danny was still in rehab.

Taylor would have accepted this assignment for purely professional reasons. Her brother's agonizing weeks in the burn ward had made it intensely personal. She was going into that friggin' island, and Mark Wolfson was going with her.

"Hybrid skin could not only save troops' lives," she said tightly, "but it could spare them months of agonizing operations. You saw what it was like in Afghanistan."

She played that trump card without batting an eye. Dr. Hayes wasn't the only scientist whose work was of vital interest to the military. Mark's own research had huge potential for battlefield application. The more a soldier could channel his or her thoughts during the chaos of battle, the more influence he or she might have on the outcome.

As a result, Mark had strapped on body armor and spent several weeks in Afghanistan as part of a team assessing the ability of both the conscious and subconscious mind to receive and process information in a hostile environment. His experience might not have been as raw and agonizing as Danny's, but he'd observed firsthand the devastation of war.

She could see she'd struck a nerve. Still holding her shoulder bag in one hand, he thrust the other through his shaggy hair. After a moment, he shook his head.

"It wouldn't work. We would have to trust each other in what sounds like a potentially dangerous situation."

"We'll make it work."

"You can't force what isn't there." Above the whiskers shadowing his cheeks, his eyes darkened to indigo. "We both learned that the hard way. Let's go. Tikal and I will walk you to your car."

Taylor stayed put. With a grunt of exasperation, Wolfson started around the coffee table.

Did he intend to physically eject her from his home? She almost wished he'd try. Knocking him on his ass might give her some long-delayed satisfaction but wouldn't exactly win his cooperation. Folding her arms, Taylor played her second and last trump card.

"Several of the research projects you're working on are funded by government grants. Seems I recall a figure in the eight to ten million dollar range. Sure would impede your work if that funding dried up."

"Are you blackmailing me, Chase?"

The soft, silky question carried such menace that Taylor jutted out her chin.

"Just stating the facts, Wolfson."

A muscle ticked in the side of his jaw. Deciding she'd given him enough to chew on, she pasted on a bland smile and rose.

"Why don't you sleep on it? I'll come to your office tomorrow morning. Ten o'clock. You can give me your answer then."

He didn't offer to walk her out again. Still smiling, she reclaimed her purse and sauntered across the room. She could feel his stare lasering into her back until the door closed behind her.

# Chapter 2

He came to her in the night.

Taylor knew it was Mark. Eight years had passed since he'd stirred her to dark, sensual passion. Eight years since he'd dragged off her sweater and unhooked her bra. Eight years since he used his hands and teeth and tongue to bring her to writhing, mindless ecstasy.

Those years could well have been mere weeks. Days. She could *feel* his presence in her hotel room. The impression was so real, so vivid he might have been looming over her bed.

"No! You're not getting into my head."

Yanking the sheet to her chin, Taylor stubbornly refused to acknowledge the sensations crawling over her skin. The tree branch that scraped against the window every time the night breeze shifted didn't help. Its faint swish gave an audible dimension to the shadows on the ceiling.

"Forget it," she told those restless patterns. "I'm not letting you in."

She hadn't intended to let him in the first time, either. It had started as a game, a challenge. The zoology prof was too serious and too absorbed in his work. Taylor had made it her personal goal to tease a smile out of him. When she'd succeeded, the results had knocked the breath back down her throat.

Dr. Mark Wolfson minus his glasses and habitual scowl looked almost human. And when his mouth tipped into a reluctant grin, damned if he didn't shed the unrelenting intensity that reduced so many of his students and lab assistants to stuttering bundles of nerves.

"Don't think about the past," Taylor said aloud, determined to banish the shadows. "Focus on the mission. Concentrate on the missing Dr. Hayes.

Think about what his research could mean to burn patients like Danny."

Despite her fierce attempt to control her thoughts, a subtle semiawareness shimmered just below the level of consciousness. Her meeting with Mark had stirred too many old memories, too many long-forgotten feelings. She couldn't shut them out of her mind. Or her body.

The sensations continued to creep over her. Slow. Dark. Insidious. Stirring her blood. Tightening her nipples.

"I won't do this! Do you hear me, Wolfson? I refuse to do this!"

The muscles low in her belly clenched. A spasm of pure sensation jolted her. Heat flushed her skin. Her breath shortened to quick, shallow pants.

She slipped her arm beneath the sheet. Her fingers slid under the elastic of her panties, over her mound, toward the aching flesh between her thighs.

"What am I doing?"

Infuriated, Taylor yanked her arm back outside the sheet.

"I won't let you influence my emotions or my actions. Not again. Do you hear me, Wolfson? Never again."

Desperate for distraction, she thought about Danny, about her last investigation, about her D.C. condo collecting dust between undercover operations. Finally she remembered a scene from the movie *Ghost*. Patrick Swayze drove Whoopi Goldberg almost out of her head singing some song over and over. What the heck was it?

Aha!

Arms rigid at her sides, the sheet wrapped around her like a shroud, Taylor belted out what she could remember of the lyrics to "I'm Henry the Eighth, I Am."

She possessed a considerable number and variety of skills. Some she'd inherited. Some she'd acquired. Unfortunately carrying a tune didn't fall into either category. Off-key and offbeat, she mangled her way through the first verse.

The tree branch banged against the window. The shadows skittered across the ceiling.

She finished the first stanza, stumbled through the chorus and started over.

She'd sung herself dry by the sixth or seventh repetition and had to get up for a glass of water. By the tenth she was croaking out each note.

\* \* \*

She woke the next morning to a scratchy throat and the fierce satisfaction of knowing she'd blocked the Wolf's attempts to invade her mind. For the sake of her mission, it was absolutely vital she remain in control of her thoughts and actions.

The assurance she could keep him out of her head boosted Taylor's confidence by exponential degrees. With grateful thanks to old "'Enery the Eighth," she plugged in the coffeepot in her hotel room and headed for the shower.

Thank God for the wizards at Kute Kutz, she thought as she blow-dried her hair. Two or three strokes of a brush and what used to be an unruly tangle of dark auburn fell into a smooth cap that followed the curve of her jaw. After adding a touch of blush and swipe of lip-gloss, she slipped into a pair of black wool slacks, a rust-colored blouse and a gray blazer.

Her next order of business was to provide her boss a status report. Coffee mug in hand, she flipped up the lid of a mobile phone packed with the latest in high-tech encryption. A special code linked her directly to OSI headquarters at Andrews Air Force Base.

"Colonel Albright's office."

"Hi, Mary. This is Captain Chase. I need to talk to the boss."

The colonel's ever-efficient executive assistant put her through immediately. Albright's booming bass assaulted Taylor's ears a moment later.

"Speak!"

Colonel Harry Albright didn't waste time *or* words. As head of the OSI's Research and Technology Protection Division, he directed a host of investigative activities designed to safeguard air force programs, critical information, personnel and facilities. Taylor had worked for him for two years now and couldn't have asked for a better—or more demanding—boss.

"Initial contact went as expected," she reported. "Wolfson refused to cooperate at first. He bent a little after I told him what kind of project Hayes was working on for us."

Not to mention her less-than-subtle reference to his government grants.

"I'm meeting him at his office at ten. If necessary, I'll twist his arm a little harder then. Once I secure his cooperation, it shouldn't take me more than a day to get up-to-speed on his current work."

"Keep me posted. As soon as you give the green light, Mary will lay on a plane to fly you and Wolfson down to the Caribbean."

"Yes, sir."

"I've tapped Staff Sergeant John Powell to handle your comm. and act as liaison in St. Kitts. You've worked with him before."

"Yes, sir, I have. He's one of the best."

"You'll need it," Albright said tersely before cutting the connection.

Sliding the cell phone into her purse, Taylor checked her watch. She still had two hours to kill before her meeting with Mark. She might as well treat herself to something more substantial than her usual power bar for breakfast.

Bright sunshine countered the September morning chill as Taylor strolled the few blocks from her hotel to the pancake house she'd spotted when she'd driven through town last night. It was located on Nassau Street, Princeton's main thoroughfare. Quaint stores and tea shops fronted one side of the historic street. The gothic towers and spires of the university dominated the other.

PJ's Pancake House was obviously a local

favorite. Students and tweed-jacketed faculty sat elbow to elbow with businessmen and women in suits. The clatter of plates and hum of conversation mingled with the tantalizing scents of fresh-brewed coffee and sizzling bacon.

Taylor lucked out and got a small table by the window after only a few minutes' wait. Her first bite of the restaurant's signature blueberry bran pancakes explained the crowd. They made the intake of fiber taste like a trip to gastronomic heaven.

The place emptied out with the start of the work and academic day, so she lingered over a second cup of coffee until almost nine forty-five. Well fortified, she paid the tab and strolled across Nassau Street to the Princeton University Visitors' Center.

The attendant at the desk verified her ID and appointment with Dr. Wolfson before issuing a visitor's pass and calling for a student to escort her across campus. Although the university covered too many acres to rigidly control access to them all, the pass showed Taylor was authorized to enter its various facilities.

The grad student who arrived some moments

later introduced herself as Meredith Sanders. The slender brunette reminded Taylor of herself a decade ago. Wearing trim slacks and a cream-colored sweater sporting Princeton's signature black and orange shield on the pocket, she was bright, self-assured and so young she made Taylor feel ancient.

"Are you familiar with Dr. Wolfson's work?" she asked as she led the way through the arch of a massive clock tower. Like the buildings around it, the tower resembled the bastion of a medieval castle.

"Somewhat," Taylor replied.

"Then you'll know he's one of the world's foremost experts in the field of consciousness-related physical phenomena. His experiments demonstrating the ways in which a cluster of female keyboard operators could mentally affect the response time of male operators more than a thousand miles away opened a whole new field of gender-related studies."

So he'd extended his range to a thousand miles. Interesting. When Taylor had first signed on as one of his lab assistants, he'd been studying the ability of a chimp named Betty to influence the behavior of her mate in the next room. Before Taylor quit grad school, Wolfson had extended that reach to the next building.

And let's not forget her apartment some blocks off campus, she acknowledged with a twist of her lips. He'd certainly influenced activities there.

"These are the quads," the cheerful brunette explained as she led the way through a maze of brick and gray granite buildings. "Mostly dorms and dining halls. And that's the University Chapel."

Taylor duly admired the structure adorned with flying buttresses, soaring spires and grinning gargoyles.

"It contains one of the largest and most precious stained-glass collections in the country," her guide said.

Descending another set of stairs, they left the nineteenth century behind and entered a more modern section of the campus. Graceful Greek Revival structures with white columns and pitched roofs basked in the shade of towering old oaks ablaze with fall color.

Twentieth century high-rises towered in the distance. Meredith followed a meandering walkway to one of those high-rises.

"Here we are. The Palmer Physics Laboratory."

Taylor eyed the amalgamation of ivy-covered granite and gleaming steel and glass. Some clever architect had managed to blend the two seamlessly.

The gargoyle perched above the gabled door caught her eye. This one came with a balding head and a potbelly. Brandishing a key in one hand, he toted a lightning bolt in the other.

"Is that supposed to be Ben Franklin?"

"It is," Meredith replied with a grin. "Ben didn't graduate from Princeton, but we've adopted him as our own. Rumor is the old dog's expression is modeled after the one he wore when Mrs. Franklin caught him sneaking in after a bout of late-night drinking at Faunce's Tavern."

Now that she mentioned it, Ben did look somewhat startled and more than a little guilty.

"There's a companion gargoyle of Teddy Roosevelt on the south gable," the brunette commented as she keyed the entry door. "You should see the expression on *his* face."

The university's architects might lean toward the fanciful and irreverent on the exteriors of its facilities, Taylor thought as she stepped into a soaring, three-story foyer, but they took their physics seriously. The directory just inside the door listed offices and labs dedicated to the study of everything from acoustics to nuclear spectroscopy.

The Physical Anomalies Research Center occupied the south wing of the third floor.

"Mark—Dr. Wolfson—is conducting a remote perception study. He asked me to take you to the observation room."

Remote perception. Mental telepathy. Psychokinesis.

Despite the varying labels and general skepticism surrounding psychic research, it wasn't a new field of study. The Defense Department had made repeated attempts to harness mental energy for military purposes. As Taylor had learned during her OSI indoctrination, the U.S. had employed a small army of clairvoyants to collect intelligence on Soviet and Chinese weapons systems during the Cold War era. These psychic warriors produced some staggering, if controversial, results.

Even today, intelligence agencies with access to the world's most sophisticated technology were still exploring alternate methods of gathering information. Infowar.Con, the world's largest conference on cyberterrorism, information warfare and critical infrastructure protection, now included a full day seminar on psychic intelligence gathering. Taylor was anxious to see firsthand what progress Mark had made in the field since their U of M days.

Cutting through a labyrinth of offices and labs, Meredith opened the door to a dimly lit booth. Computers with flickering screens lined a low counter. A glass wall separated the booth from a brightly illuminated lab.

"The glass is one-way," Meredith assured Taylor, "and soundproof. They can't see or hear us."

"They" were the four men in the lab. Mark and two white-coated assistants were grouped on one side of a small table. A beefy, middle-aged man in tan slacks and an open-necked sport shirt sat across from them. Sensors had been applied to his major pulse points. Cameras were positioned to record him from every angle.

"Mr. Bailey is a local Realtor. His wife claims he frequently experiences déjà vulike episodes and talked him into volunteering for this series of experiments. He's our percipient."

The person or animal on the receiving end of a

mental communication, Taylor translated. Wolfson had labeled them receptors at Michigan.

"Our agent is a forty-three-year-old tour bus operator in Rabat, Morocco."

Agent, she guessed, was the new term for transmitter.

"He's one of six volunteers with demonstrated extrasensory skills recruited by our colleague at the University of Rabat. The bus driver has randomly selected a scene to view and describe in his own words. Our colleague is documenting both his description and what he's actually seeing via a video satellite hookup. Let's listen while Mr. Bailey receives mental imagery from the bus driver in Morocco."

She flicked a switch and filled the booth with the percipient's hesitant description.

"...not sure. It's a sort of half oval. Like an arch or something. It's decorated in a geometric pattern, with really bright colors. Turquoise and white and gold."

Lips pursed, the Realtor stared at a point above and beyond Mark's left shoulder.

"There's someone standing near the arch. I think

he's a soldier. He's wearing boots and a red uniform and a hat. It looks... Hell, it looks like a turban."

The three observers facing the percipient didn't register so much as a flicker of emotion, but Taylor's escort used the soundproofing to let loose with a delighted whoop.

"He's nailed it. Look!"

She angled a flat screen monitor around for Taylor to view. The display showed a turbaned grenadier in a crimson uniform slashed by a white belt. His rifle shouldered, he stood at stiff attention outside the entrance to an ornate hall.

As the women watched, he executed a left face and marched at a slow tread toward a similarly uniformed soldier. The two met in the center of an arch ablaze with colorful mosaic tiles and brought their right arms across their chests in a stiff salute. Executing an about-face, they returned to their original positions.

"They're part of an honor guard." With unrestrained glee, Meredith read the text scrolling across the screen. "They stand watch at the tomb of King Mohammed the Fifth."

A shiver rippled down Taylor's spine. Wolfson really *had* made significant strides in mental transference and remote influencing. If he could translate his research into practical applications, the implications were staggering.

She remained silent until he terminated the experiment some time later. While his assistants removed the percipient's sensors, Mark stood at the table, unmoving. At first Taylor thought he was simply gathering his thoughts on the experiment. Then he lifted his head and locked his gaze on the window to the observation booth.

Another shiver danced across Taylor's skin. He couldn't see her. He knew she was here, but he couldn't spot her through the one-way glass. Succumbing to a ridiculous impulse, she stuck out her tongue.

Wolfson's scientific objectivity evaporated. A grin spread across his face, making him appear years younger, and the sound of a rich chuckle reverberated through the booth's built-in speakers.

His assistants gaped at him in astonishment. Meredith, too, appeared stunned. She'd missed Taylor's lapse into childishness, thank goodness, and didn't have a clue what had provoked Mark's reaction.

He covered it by shaking Bailey's hand. "Thanks, Jack. That was an excellent session."

"Yeah? Did I see what the other guy saw, Doc?"

"I'll let you know after we review the video imagery and perform a detailed analysis. Meredith, will you escort Mr. Bailey back across campus?"

Taylor waited in the booth while Mark and his other two assistants reviewed the video on a terminal in the lab. Mark let them revel in the results for several minutes before tempering their jubilation with a word of caution.

"We're still a long way from sufficient documentary evidence to present at the Chicago conference. We need to dictate the results of this experiment and start defining the parameters for the next."

He stuffed his notes in a leather portfolio and exited the lab. When he joined Taylor in the booth, she was ready for him. Or thought she was.

Raising a brow, he skimmed a glance over her face. "You look a little ragged around the edges. Rough night?"

"Not at all. I slept like a baby."

"Is that so?"

To her disgust, he whistled the chorus to the song she'd belted out last night. In key, dammit!

Taylor refused to acknowledge that he'd scored a hit and hitched a hip on the counter. "Your subject gave an impressive performance just now."

"Bailey's an excellent percipient. Incredible what the man can see."

"Do you think we could ask him to describe the facilities on a certain island in the Caribbean?"

Interest flared in his face, only to die a moment later.

"It wouldn't work. We'd need an agent on the island, someone viewing a particular scene and focusing his thoughts on it."

"Couldn't Dr. Hayes be the agent? Bailey could attempt to see whatever Hayes sees."

"He could try, but we'd have no way of validating his perceptions without an unbiased observer."

"I'm not talking a rigidly controlled scientific experiment here, Mark. We've got satellite imagery of the island and its buildings. What I need—what *we* need—is a sense of what we'll find when we get inside those buildings."

He noted the deliberate use of the plural but didn't contradict her. Taylor was sure then that she had him.

"It's worth a try," he conceded. "I don't want

to use university facilities, however, as this experiment doesn't fall within the parameters of our approved protocol."

She could hardly miss the pointed reference to their past. Her allegation that he'd conducted an unauthorized experiment with her as the subject hovered between them. Taylor shrugged it aside.

"We can do it at your place. Or my hotel room. This afternoon or evening, if possible. We need to jump a plane to the Caribbean tomorrow. Next day at the latest."

"Right. The Caribbean." He cocked his head. "You really intend to go through with the crazy plan to scuttle a sailboat and wade ashore on a heavily guarded private island?"

"I've done crazier things in my life."

*Like falling for an uptight zoology professor who played me like one of Pavlov's dogs.*

Too late Taylor tried to censor the thought. Mark's face went as hard and as flat as his reply.

"I'll let you know what Bailey says."

# Chapter 3

She'd fallen for him all those years ago?

Mark mulled over Taylor's mental slip as he crossed the campus that evening. Her hotel was on Nassau Street, only a short walk through an autumn night tinged with the scent of burning leaves. A blast of frigid arctic air had swept down from Canada during the afternoon. September would go out in style.

Shoulders hunched under his tweed sport coat, Mark shoved his hands in his pockets and buried his chin in the wool muffler wrapped twice around his throat. He still couldn't make sense of it.

Taylor had fallen for him? How had he missed the signs?

He held a Ph.D. in zoology, for God's sake. Before a simple experiment involving the parallel behavior of rats caged in separate rooms had propelled him out of zoology and into the field of consciousness-related research, he'd acquired a vast reservoir of knowledge of the animal world. His personal database included gender-specific sexual patterns on just about every species known to man.

Unfortunately all that expertise on animal reproductive behaviors had failed to prepare him for the kick to his gut the first time a certain green-eyed grad student had flashed him a smile.

What had begun with a simple, flirtatious ruffling of tail feathers soon evolved into a full-fledged mating ritual. As the semester progressed, the air around Mark and his assistant had almost crackled with all the endorphins they'd shot off like sparks.

There was never any question in his mind that the attraction had been mutual. He knew damned well Taylor had lusted for him as much as he had for her. Yet she'd wrapped her desire in laughter and playful sexual banter. He'd never suspected she'd *fallen* for him.

What the devil did that mean, anyway? Where, precisely, did that vague condition rank in the wide range of human emotions? And why the hell would he feel this jolt of primitive male satisfaction at the idea that he'd stirred something more than animal hunger in Taylor?

Intelligent, intriguing, irritating Taylor.

He shouldn't be feeling anything except regret and guilt and disgust over their brief affair. It had almost destroyed his career. Worse, Taylor believed Mark had perverted his research to entice her into bed.

Maybe he had. God knew he'd wanted her badly enough. If he'd used his mind to feed her hunger, however, he hadn't done it with conscious deliberation. Not then.

Last night was a different story. Her unexpected arrival had stirred unwanted memories. And her less-than-subtle blackmail attempt had roused his fury, which he'd released in that dark, erotic bombardment.

Mark knew he'd gotten to her, physically as

well as mentally. He'd heard her breath quicken, felt her moist heat against his skin. Then she'd launched into that atrocious singing. The area in his frontal lobe that processed sound still ached from her atonal assault.

So why hadn't he cut the connection then and there? Why had he allowed Taylor access to the lab this morning? Why had he shown her around the institute?

The answer to those questions had nothing to do with government funding. He knew his research carried too many implications for the military for them to simply pull away. What he didn't know was why he'd agreed to arrange this special session with Jack Bailey tonight when he hadn't yet decided to accompany Taylor to the Caribbean.

Frowning, Mark dug his chin deeper into his muffler. The wool smelled faintly of fur. Tikal must have rolled up in it again. Wrapped in his thoughts and the familiar scent of dog, he stalked through the Nassau Street gate and left the security of his university cocoon behind.

The session with Jack Bailey produced mixed results.

They set up in the spacious sitting area of

Taylor's hotel room. Jack took the armchair by the window. Mark sat at the desk with a digital video camera aimed at the percipient. Taylor perched on the edge of her bed, well clear of the camera's viewing angle.

To her disappointment, Bailey couldn't connect with anyone inside the facilities depicted on the satellite surveillance photos. However, he did "see" a shimmering turquoise swimming pool and what he thought was a summerhouse or cabana.

"It's got white pillars. Columns, like in a Greek temple. And vines dripping big red flowers. Hibiscus or something. I think there's a woman in the cabana. A blonde."

Taylor caught Mark's quick glance and answered with a nod. Satellite reconnaissance had confirmed the presence of at least three females on the island.

"She's stretched out on a chaise lounge," Bailey continued. "I gotta tell you, this babe's a looker."

Taylor itched to ask if there was anyone with the woman, but she knew better than to intrude on a percipient's consciousness.

"I'm getting a whiff of something." The Realtor's

forehead creased. "Not flowers, although I can smell them, too. This is sort of fishy, but not quite."

Mark threw Taylor another glance. She could see the sudden speculation in his eyes. She curbed her eagerness to know what had sparked it until Bailey swiped a palm over his balding crown and ended the session.

"Sorry, Doc. That's all I got. Can you use it?"

"We can. Thanks, Jack."

"Anytime." Grinning, the beefy Realtor shrugged into his sports jacket. "My wife used to think my déjà vu episodes were just this side of weird. Now that I'm working with you, she gives them—and me—a little more credibility."

Taylor waited until he'd shaken her hand and departed to pounce. "What was that smell he described?"

"It could have originated from any number of sources."

"Com'on, Wolfson. You suspected something. What?"

"My first thought was that it rose from the sea surrounding the island." Calmly he clipped the lens cover on the digital camera. "My second was that it might be heparin."

Taylor's pulse skipped. A team from Walter Reed had given her a crash course in organ transplant procedures in preparation for this op. Heparin, she knew, was an anticlotting agent that occurred naturally in the livers of certain animals. It was used to preserve transplant organs prior to removal from a donor.

"Your turn." Mark set the camera aside. "Who's the woman Bailey described?"

"Sounds like the wife of man who owns the island. His name is Diederik van Deursen."

"Swedish?"

"Dutch. Van Deursen inherited the island from his great-great-great-whatever-granddad, one of the original colonizers of the Dutch West Indies. Granddad supposedly got rich plundering Spanish treasure galleons. Whatever the source of his family's wealth, Diederik inherited billions."

Frowning, Mark stretched out his legs and locked his hands behind his head. A favorite position when he was thinking, Taylor remembered with a sudden hitch in her breath. Before she could stop it, a memory slammed into her.

He'd been sprawled just like this, legs outstretched, arms looped behind his neck, staring at the picture of Charles Darwin on the wall of his cluttered office when Taylor stopped by. The barriers between professor and grad student had tumbled down weeks before, but still he'd been surprised when she'd hiked up her skirt and swung a leg over his. Surprise had morphed into delight when she rubbed herself against him, slowly, deliciously, before tugging down his zipper and...

"Something doesn't track."

"Wh...? What?"

"This business with van Deursen. It doesn't track."

Thank you, Lord! Swallowing her relief that Wolfson had been too preoccupied to invade her mind, Taylor planted herself firmly back in the present.

"What doesn't track?"

"Why would a man with his kind of money get involved in a scheme to engineer synthetic organs and sell them on the black market?"

"We've been asking ourselves the same question. Maybe because he *has* that kind of money. Wealth can breed its own arrogance and avarice. Or maybe he believes these organs will save the lives of desperately ill people who've been waiting for years for a transplant."

"Or maybe he sees it as an alternative to the sale of human organs that's become such a huge industry in countries like China, Brazil, India and Pakistan," Mark suggested.

Taylor wasn't sure where she came down on that issue. Proponents argued that legalizing the sale of human body parts worldwide would help regulate the flourishing organ trade in third world countries, where a poor villager might receive five or six thousand dollars for a liver that was then sold for upwards of fifty thousand to a wealthy recipient. Supposedly universal legalization would also allow for closer scrutiny of the hundreds of transplants being performed daily on those who could afford to fly to India or Singapore or South Africa for the operation.

After watching what her brother went through over the past eighteen months, all Taylor knew was that she'd do whatever she could to help others avoid that kind of suffering. Right now, that narrowed down to finding out why Dr. Oscar Hayes was on Diederik van Deursen's private island and, if necessary, arranging his extraction.

"I can't speculate on why van Deursen may be involved in the organ trade. I *can* confirm that satellite imagery of his island showed a cluster of buildings that look suspiciously like research facilities. The National Intelligence Center kept it on their watch list until Dr. Hayes disappeared. That's when the air force got involved."

"And you."

"And me," she agreed. "Now you."

"Maybe." Wolfson didn't alter his loose-limbed sprawl. "I still haven't decided to head south."

His waffling caught Taylor by surprise. "I thought... I assumed when you showed me around your lab and briefed me on your latest research it was a done deal."

"You should know better than to make assumptions without empirical evidence to support them."

"So you've just been stringing me along, Wolfson? Again?"

Unlocking his hands, he thrust out of the desk chair with a fluid grace that reminded Taylor forcefully of his dog's response when she attempted to sit up last night. The male who confronted her now appeared no less intimidating.

"Let's get one thing straight. If I decide to accompany you to the Caribbean, it won't be because of any government grants. Or," he added with a nasty smile, "because I'm hoping for a repeat of your spectacular performance that afternoon in my office at U of M."

Dammit all to hell! She was positive he hadn't locked onto that erotic little brain fart. As heat rushed into her cheeks, Taylor swore to do a better job at keeping a lid on her memories.

"Then what *would* induce you to go?" she asked icily.

"Some proof Oscar is being held on that island against his will, for a start."

"I told you, we don't know that."

Mark folded his arms, his face hard. "Oscar has a wife."

"His wife died two years ago."

"What about his daughter? His grandson? Surely he's been in touch with them."

He was too close. Taylor could see the bristly beginnings of a five o'clock shadow, the faint threads of silver at his temples. Needing some space, she pushed past him and went to the minibar to twist the cap off a bottle of water.

When she offered it to Mark, he declined with an impatient shake of his head. She downed several swallows before replying to his rapid-fire inquisition.

"Dr. Hayes has spoken with his daughter a couple of times by phone. She thinks he's taking a long-overdue vacation, courtesy of one of the rich philanthropists who sponsor his research."

"So why does the air force think differently?"

"Would you just up and walk away from a project you'd worked on day and night for almost two years? One that might impact the treatment of millions of desperately ill people?"

Mark knew what his response should be. The warnings ricocheted around in his head like shrapnel.

*Back away from her.*

*She turned your world upside down once.*

*She'll do it again.*

If he had one tenth of the intelligence he was credited with, he'd heed those warnings. Just a few hours in Taylor's company had stirred memories he'd buried years ago. Not to mention latent instincts he never knew he possessed. This fierce, primal urge to drag her down onto the bed, roll her over and mount her might be appropriate behavior for Tikal, but not for...

Oh, hell! Tikal.

Jerked back to reality, Mark shoved a hand through his hair. If he went traipsing off to the Caribbean with Taylor, what would he do with the dog? The few times he'd asked one of his assistants or colleagues to look after the animal had led to near disaster. Not even the bubbly, cheerful Meredith would get within nipping range. Tikal didn't take kindly to outsiders invading his territory.

An impatient clicking drew his gaze to Taylor's hand. Clearly tired of waiting, she was tapping a nail against the plastic water bottle.

"Don't waste any more of my time, Wolfson. Are you in or not?"

He pulled in a long breath and shut down those warning voices in his head. "I'm in."

"Good. We'll need to..."

"On one condition."

Instantly, obviously wary, she asked, "What?"

"My dog goes with us."

"Wrong! Your dog almost ripped out my throat. No way I'm sharing a small boat with something who regards me as the next best thing to hamburger."

"First, you tripped over your own feet. Tikal didn't attack or inflict bodily harm."

"Yeah, well, he wanted to."

"Second, his aggressiveness could come in useful if we have to fight our way off the island."

"That's what guns are for," she muttered, unconvinced.

"Third, Tikal could constitute an added set of eyes and ears. He can sniff out things we'd miss."

"His sniffer won't do him *or* us much good if the tropical heat gets to him. His coat is as thick as a polar bear's."

"That's a specious argument and you know it. His woolly undercoat provides as much insulation from heat as it does from cold."

Taylor liked dogs. She really did. She'd have a mutt of her own if her job didn't require her to travel so much. She just didn't particularly care for half-wild breeds with fangs that would rouse the envy of a saber-toothed tiger.

"If I go," Mark stated, folding his arms, "Tikal goes."

"Okay, okay! But you have to clean up after him when he poops on the deck."

For the second time that day, amusement sparked in his blue eyes. The first, Taylor recalled, was when she'd stuck out her tongue behind a supposedly impenetrable shield. That prompted her to impose a few conditions of her own.

"Before we close this deal, I want some concessions from you."

His laughter faded. "I'm listening."

"First, you stay out of my head."

"You could always sing. Or attempt to."

"Two, we put the past behind us once and for all."

The blunt suggestion brought him up short. "How do you propose we accomplish that?"

"We start over. Right here, right now. As colleagues and…"

Taylor hesitated a few seconds, acknowledging how difficult it would be for either of them to bury the past. Yet they didn't have a prayer of accomplishing their mission unless they worked as a team. With that thought firmly in mind, she thrust out her hand.

"As colleagues and friends."

The emotion that flickered across his face came and went so swiftly she couldn't read it.

"All right. We start now." His hand folded around hers. "Friends and colleagues."

His grip was too strong for a man who'd spent most of his adult life in a laboratory, and too familiar for Taylor's peace of mind. Keeping an artificial smile firmly in place, she eased her hand out of his.

"I'll notify my boss and tell him we're good to go. Can you and, uh, Tikal, be ready by 8:00 a.m.?"

"It'll take some arranging, but we'll manage."

"I'll lay on an airlift down to St. Kitts. From there it's not more than a five- or six-hour sail to van Deursen's island."

He nodded, but the expression on his face gave rise to a sudden wave of doubt.

"Can you handle anything larger than a sunfish?" she asked.

"That depends. What's a sunfish?"

Taylor dragged a deep breath. Okay. All right. No problem. She could take care of the water phase of their operation herself.

True, she'd sailed the Caribbean only once before. But she'd been born and bred on Michigan's Upper Peninsula. She and her brothers had kayaked and canoed endlessly where the waters of Lakes Huron, Superior and Michigan met and mingled. They'd also pestered their dad until he purchased a used catamaran, which they'd sent skimming under the arches of the Mackinaw Bridge.

Unless a tropical storm or hurricane blew in without warning, the short sail from St. Kitts to van Deursen's island should be the equivalent of an aquatic walk in the park.

# Chapter 4

Taylor and Mark flew into Basseterre, the capital of St. Kitts.

Ringed by lush green hills, the city retained vestiges of its colonial past in a dome-topped Customs House and buildings constructed in elegant, Georgian-style architecture. After the nipping cold of New Jersey, the breeze that rustled through palms around the harbor felt like warm silk against Taylor's skin. She shed her blazer and Mark his tweed sport coat during the drive in from the airport.

A two-man advance team was waiting when they arrived at the marina in Basseterre's main harbor. As promised, Colonel Albright had sent USAF Staff Sergeant John Powell to handle communications. Constable Nigel Benjamin, the police officer assigned as their liaison, would provide necessary coordination with local authorities.

"Good to see you again, Captain Chase."

Also an OSI field agent, Powell had worked an op with Taylor two years ago, when they'd both been assigned to Izmir AB, Turkey.

"You, too, John. This is Dr. Mark Wolfson."

Powell stuck out his hand, but yanked it back when the animal that had accompanied them to St. Kitts issued an abrupt warning.

"Sorry." Mark stroked the dog's ruff. "This is Sergeant Powell, Tikal. He's a friend."

The constable kept a safe distance until Mark had vetted him, too. Big and bluff, with features derived from both his native Carib heritage and from ancestors imported as slaves to work the sugar plantations, Benjamin squatted down and let the dog come to him.

"So you're the bloke I had to work the special

entry permit for. Going for a sail and a bit of a swim, are you?"

Tikal's tail executed a condescending half-swish before he hunkered down at Mark's side. Keeping a wary eye on the dog, Sergeant Powell passed Taylor a set of keys and nodded to the boat moored in a slip near the end of the dock.

"That's her. The *Island Breeze*."

From where Taylor stood, it looked as though the twenty-eight-foot sloop-rigged Pearson had logged more than its fair share of sea days. Her fiberglass hull was patched in several spots and rust rimmed the casing of the outboard engine. Her teak rails had been lovingly sanded and varnished, however, and Constable Benjamin assured Taylor the navigation equipment was more than adequate.

"Nigel here has fueled her and stocked the galley with everything a couple would need for a two-week cruise around the Leeward Islands," Sergeant Powell said. "You want to stow your gear and check her out before we confer?"

While the two men waited inside the marina, Tikal explored the boat's unfamiliar scents and Taylor and Mark took turns using the sloop's small, V-shaped cabin to change into clothing more suitable for the tropics.

She traded her wool slacks and blouse for shorts, a cotton tank top, and rubber-soled boat shoes. The canvas shoes were slip-ons, but had laces that tied around the ankle to keep them from coming loose when she went into the water. They'd also been specially modified for this mission.

Mark emerged from below in cutoffs, flip-flops, and a sleeveless Princeton exercise tank in various shades of faded orange. Its oversize armholes and wide strip of perforated netting at the midriff were perfect for letting in the sea breeze. They also gave Taylor an unobstructed view of a flat abdomen and broad shoulders roped with sinewy muscles.

Whoa! Where had that all-over tan come from? Surely the introverted, reclusive Professor Wolfson wasn't into tanning salons?

"It's Tikal," he said absently. "He requires regular exercise. We jog five or six miles every morning."

"Dammit, Wolfson!"

Her furious outburst whipped him around. "What?"

"You *promised* to stay out of my head."

"Oh. Right." Chagrined, he hooked his thumbs in the front pockets of his cutoffs. "Sorry."

She might have accepted his apology if he hadn't followed up with a terse comment.

"It *is* a two-way communication, you know. I can't receive signals you don't transmit."

"So I'm supposed to completely shut down my thought processes?"

"No, of course not." He hesitated before offering a tentative solution. "We've been testing a portal technique at the institute."

"What kind of portal?" she asked suspiciously.

"A gateway that would allow percipients to filter out selected agents."

"You mean a mechanism I could use to keep you out?"

"More or less."

The qualification gave Taylor pause. Wolfson had experimented on her once. Granted, she'd been a willing participant in the sexual dance preceding the experiment. Okay, more than willing. She'd made most of the initial moves.

Naive fool that she was, Taylor just never imagined he would play on her own thoughts to get her into bed. Or that he would document her physiological and emotional responses to their explosive mating.

"I never intended to document your responses," he said quietly. "They just astounded me, Taylor. *You* astounded me. I merely wanted to…"

"That tears it," she interrupted, grinding her teeth. "As soon as we finish with Powell and Benjamin and take the *Island Breeze* for a trial run, you teach me this portal technique."

They spent the next two hours with their two-man support team. Appropriating the marina's back office, they went over the details of the operations plan, scrutinized the latest satellite imagery of Diederik van Deursen's facilities and detailed what they knew of the man himself.

It wasn't much. Reclusive by nature, van Deursen spent a good chunk of his billions to guard his privacy. Intelligence had pulled together a brief bio and a detailed analysis of his financial holdings. Nothing in either gave Taylor a good feel for the forty-three-year-old Dutchman who'd managed to keep the paparazzi off his tail even during his whirlwind courtship and marriage to a twenty-something high school dropout from south Texas.

The photos Intel had supplied of a young Beverly van Deursen intrigued Taylor's three male counterparts as much as Beverly's mental image had Jack Bailey. The tall, stacked blond had Mark's brows lifting and Sergeant Powell's lips pursing in a silent whistle.

Before taking a break, Powell gave Taylor the communications device he'd rigged especially for this operation. The cell phone was wafer thin and would fit into a concealed compartment in the insole of her left shoe.

"It may look like an ordinary cell phone," he said as Taylor hefted the featherweight instrument in her palm, "but you can run over it with a steamroller or drop it from a twenty-story building and this baby will still send encrypted transmissions."

"How about taking it down with a sinking ship?"

"That, too."

"You sure van Deursen's men won't intercept our transmissions?"

A pained expression crossed Powell's face. "I'm sure. The device can send voice, data or text transmissions as well as coded signals. It also acts as an electronic sweep."

"Excellent," Taylor murmured.

"I've programmed the device to recognize your fingerprint and heat signature," Powell continued. "Press the star key and hold it for two seconds to indicate situation under control. Press it three times in rapid succession to signal duress. Hit star six to contact me directly. The number key activates the electronic sweeper."

"Got it."

Slipping off her shoe, Taylor peeled back the inner lining and inserted the phone into its nest.

"I'll give it a try when we take the sloop out for a trial run. Which we need to do while we still have some daylight."

"Good enough." Constable Benjamin hooked his thumb toward a thatched-roof restaurant at the far side of the harbor. "We'll meet you at the Blue Parrot for a final review. It's noisy and crowded, but it serves the best conch chowder on the island."

Before taking the *Island Breeze* out of its slip, Taylor tested the onboard equipment and gave Mark a crash course in marine safety and navigation. By the time they threw off the mooring lines and backed out of the slip, it was late afternoon. Plenty of time to see how the sloop handled and feel the wind on their faces.

Tikal gained his sea legs before they cleared the marina. His claws noisy on the fiberglass deck, the dog scrambled forward and assumed lookout duties. Every swooping gull and scudding harbor seal earned a round of fierce barks.

"You see those navigation beacons?" Taylor pitched her voice above the din and directed Mark's attention to a set of channel markers. "Always keep the green markers on your left, or port, side when going out to sea and the red to starboard—right—when returning."

"Left, port, going out," Mark repeated. "Right, starboard, coming in."

"Sailor's use a simple phrase. Just remember Red, Right, Returning."

"Red, Right, Returning. Got it."

"Notice how some markers are shaped like buoys, some like cans, and others are triangular or square. The shape signals depth or a possible hazard. And each has a number that corresponds to the numbers on your navigational charts."

The harbor breeze ruffled Mark's black hair as he spread the chart on the hatch cover and studied it with single-minded intensity.

This is a switch, Taylor mused. The student is now instructing the professor. Although... She had to admit she'd taught Professor Wolfson more than one interesting move before their affair blew up in...

Stop! Don't go there! Don't open the damned portal!

Pursing her lips, she started to whistle the melody to "Henry the Eighth."

The shrill notes brought Mark's head around. Taylor responded to his surprised look with a bland smile and another verse. Shaking his head, he returned his attention to the chart.

Ha! Take that Wolfson!

Still whistling, she relaxed and turned her attention to the wind and blazing sun. Sweat soon pearled on her upper lip. The engine vibrated through the deck under her feet. Gauging the boat's pitch and roll, she kept it under power until they cleared the harbor channel.

"Time to raise sail," she announced, cutting the

engine. "I'll show you how to work the sheets and shrouds."

She should have known Mark would approach sailing with a scientist's need for precise detail. She did her best to respond to his questions about the ratio of sail yardage to wind thrust. At his request, she drew a detailed diagram of the sailing quadrant and pointed out the various angles for sailing close-hauled and breach-hauled.

Her head started to hurt when he calculated the drag on the block and pulleys used to raise the sail, however. Finally she begged for mercy.

"Enough with the Physics 303. Please, just haul on that halyard."

Shrugging, he tipped two fingers to his brow. "Aye, aye, Captain."

Even Tikal wanted in on the act. Abandoning lookout duty, he clicked over to Taylor and watched curiously while she set the jib. Evidently she provided a tempting target. When she bent to tie the sheet to the forward clew, he goosed her with a cold, wet nose.

"Hey!" Startled, she jerked upright. "Watch where you stick that, pal."

Tail swishing, the silver-maned Husky returned

her glare with a look of such devilish enjoyment
that she suspected he'd pulled that stunt before.
Mark's snort of suppressed laughter confirmed
her suspicions.

The sun hovered just above St. Kitts's lush
peaks when they tacked back into the harbor.

Taylor had made sure they stayed within sight
of land while she taught basic seamanship. Both
man and dog had proven themselves quick
learners. Mark had experienced only one near
miss with the swinging boom. And Tikal had discovered that leaping joyously into a passing
school of snapper was a whole lot easier than
climbing back aboard with a flapping fish in his
jaws.

Sweaty, wind-reddened and hungry, they nosed
the *Island Breeze* back into its slip. Once moored,
they reeled out a dock hose and washed down
deck, dog and each other.

Taylor checked her watch. They'd agreed to
meet Powell and Benjamin at 7:00 p.m. They'd
just make it. Luckily her shorts were drip-dry and
her cotton tank top contained a built-in bra. A

quick finger-comb of her wet hair and she was good to go.

"Ready to chow down?" she asked Mark.

He skimmed a hand over his dripping cutoffs and the wet athletic shirt molding his chest. "Like this?"

"Welcome to the laid-back world of sailing. What about Tikal? Should we shut him in below?"

"He's okay here on deck."

"You sure? He's jumped ship once already."

Mark glanced at the animal. Tikal angled his head in question.

"We'll bring you dinner," Mark promised.

Nigel Benjamin was already at the palm-thatched restaurant with its wide-open view of the harbor. He'd changed out of his uniform and now wore shorts and a shirt sprinkled with palms and parrots. Clutching a dew-streaked bottle of the local brew, he'd tipped his chair back and was jiggling a sandaled foot to the rhythm of steel drums.

"How did the boat handle?"

"Beautifully. Too bad we have to scuttle her."

"All in the line of duty."

The lively calypso beat, buzz of conversation

and noisy clatter from the kitchen provided the perfect shield for their conversation. Not that Taylor suspected any of the shorts-and-sandals types crowding the other tables of having them under visual or audio surveillance. Still, she angled her chair to put her back to the wall and give a clear view of the approach to their table.

"Did you dig up any more information on the number of staff employed on van Deursen's island?" she asked Nigel.

"Matter of fact, I did. One of our Basseterre girls works as a cook's helper. I found out she came home to tend her sick granny. Van Deursen makes his employees sign a nondisclosure statement, so Thérèse was a bit reluctant to chat with me at first, but I convinced her to give an accounting of the number of meals they dish up each day."

The constable and Taylor put their heads together over cold beers and were still discussing the staff numbers when Sergeant Powell arrived. He, too, had gone native. His baggy shorts came to midcalf and his tropical shirt rivaled Benjamin's for garish color. There was no mistaking his military buzz-cut, though, or the dead seriousness of his expression as the constable briefed him on the revised estimate of guards patrolling van Deursen's island.

Dinner consisted of conch chowder, banana fritters and another round of cold beer. Taylor and her team reassessed the risks as they ate. Mark spooned his creamy stew, listening intently but saying little.

"I'll go in unarmed, as planned," Taylor concluded after some discussion. "I can't conceal a weapon in wet shorts and a tank top. If necessary, I'll appropriate one from van Deursen's boys."

Appropriate? Christ!

Mark barely recognized the laughing, irreverent grad student who'd turned his world upside down in this cool, precise government agent. He'd caught a glimpse of the younger Taylor on the boat this afternoon. With the wind whipping her hair and her face raised to the sun, she'd delivered a kick to his gut he hadn't expected or been prepared for.

This talk of disarming van Deursen's guards and shooting her way off his island delivered another sucker punch. It was one thing to discuss the possibility of danger two or three thousand miles away, another to have it waiting for you across a few nautical miles of open sea. Wondering what the hell he'd gotten himself into, Mark finished his dinner and ordered a rare steak to go for Tikal.

Once back at the marina, Benjamin wished them luck and departed. Powell lingered for a private conversation with Taylor. Mark had moved down the dock, but snatches of it carried across the water.

"I heard about your brother, Captain Chase. How's he doing?"

"It was touch and go for a while, but he pulled through."

"Friggin' IEDs."

"Yeah."

"Well, good luck with Hayes and van Deursen. From all indications, you'll need it."

"Thanks."

Mark was rooted where he stood. When Taylor started down the dock, he blocked her way.

"What was that about your brother?"

"Did you crawl into my head again?"

"I overheard you and Powell. Tell me about your brother."

He knew she had two—one older, one younger—and that her parents were both school teachers in Michigan's Upper Peninsula. That was pretty much the extent of the personal information he and Taylor had exchanged during their mating dance. They'd had far more pressing matters on their mind at the time.

"Tell me."

"Danny's a marine," she bit out. "Or was until his HumVee triggered a roadside bomb last year and the whole vehicle ignited. He's been in and out of the burn ward ever since."

The revelation rocked Mark back on his heels. He should have realized her stake in this operation went beyond professional.

"Is that why you're so dead set on hauling Oscar Hayes back to the States? Because the project he was working for the air force could help alleviate your brother's agony?"

"No! Okay, yes. But what happened to Danny doesn't alter the parameters of this mission."

"The hell it doesn't! You know as well as I do emotion directly impacts the ability of our conscious mind to receive and process information."

"You learn to control your emotions in my

line of work, Wolfson. It's a necessary condition for survival."

"You may think you can stuff them in a box…"

"I know I can. Otherwise I wouldn't be here. With you," she added pointedly.

Mark's jaw tightened. Did she really believe she could shut him out? The idea was as ridiculous as her proposal that they put the past behind them. It was right there, in the angle of her chin as she tossed him a terse out.

"You want off this operation? You'd better tell me now if you do. Once we weigh anchor tomorrow morning, I'm not turning back."

Hell, yes, he wanted off. He wasn't Princeton's version of Rambo. He didn't feel the least need to prove his masculinity by taking on van Deursen's private army. And he'd never bought into that old cliché about danger being the ultimate aphrodisiac. All empirical evidence pointed to the exact opposite.

What's more, he didn't believe for a minute Taylor's flat assertion she could separate the personal from the professional. She wouldn't believe it, either, if she'd devoted as many years as he had to the influence of mind over matter.

He probably would have called it quits at that point if not for the absolute certainly she would storm van Deursen's island with *or* without him.

"I've come this far," he bit out. "I'll go the rest of the way."

She accepted his decision with a curt nod. "Let's feed your dog. Then you're going to teach me this portal business."

Tikal wolfed down the steak in two bites. Licking his chops, he joined Mark and Taylor in the small galley belowdecks. It was fitted with a built-in bench, a stow-away table, a sink and the cupboards Constable Benjamin had stocked. A rack of radio and navigational equipment was attached to one bulkhead. A narrow bunk folded down on the other.

Mark sat on the bunk. Taylor faced him across the narrow table. They'd carried the residue of their confrontation on the dock with them. Tikal picked up on the tension and pattered the cramped cabin restlessly before flopping down near the steps leading to the open hatch.

"I'm ready," Taylor announced tersely.

"The technique sounds simple, but it's worked

for a good number of our percipients in a controlled environment."

"Which this isn't."

"Granted. Close your eyes and imagine a gate."

"What kind?"

"Any kind."

Forehead creasing, she did as instructed. The first gate that came to mind was the heavily guarded entrance to the Green Zone in Baghdad. Sandbagged and bristling with gun emplacements, the zigzagging concrete barrier blocked traffic coming in and going out.

It took a few moments to envision a second, less menacing image. Taylor had almost forgotten the shed tucked at the back of her grandparents' home. Over the years the wooden building had done duty as stable, woodworking shop and storage shed. Its half-door had creaked on rusty hinges whenever Taylor or her brothers snuck inside to explore the stalls crammed with the remnants of a past era.

"Okay. I've got a gate."

"Is it open or shut?"

"Shut."

"Open it."

The hinges screeched a protest. "Done."

"Now envision someone standing on the other side."

"Someone?"

"The person or entity you want to keep from entering your portal."

She raised one eyelid, skewered him with a sharp glance and squeezed her eye shut again. "Got him."

"Now close the gate."

"Did you hear it slam?"

He huffed out an exasperated breath. "Do you want this to work or not?"

"If you're asking if I want you on the other side of a mental barrier, you know the answer."

"Then cut the sarcasm and focus."

She was silent for a moment. "Okay. I'm there."

"Lock the gate."

The rusty bolt slid into its hasp. "Done."

"Now open your eyes."

When Mark swam into focus, Taylor waited for his next instruction. There was none.

"That's it?" she asked skeptically. "That's your portal technique?"

"That's it."

She shook her head. "All those millions in research grants and the best that you can come up with is 'shut the gate'?"

"Let's just hope it works," Mark retorted, his professional pride pricked. "My ears can't take another of your audible assaults."

"Excuse me, but some of us don't have perfect pitch."

"Some of us don't have any pitch at all. You want to flip to see who gets the cabin and who gets this bunk?"

"You and Tikal can have the cabin. I'll sleep up on deck. It's cooler, and I'm used to it. Just let me take a quick shower and I'll be out of your hair."

It would take more than a shower to accomplish that, Mark thought as he and Tikal meandered along the sandy beach edging the harbor. After the dog had lifted his leg a sufficient number of times to leave an indelible mark on St. Kitts, they returned to the *Island Breeze*.

Tikal descended the cabin stairs with a loud bark announcing his return. Mark followed more slowly and met Taylor on the way up.

She'd changed into clean shorts and a cotton

T-shirt. This one was sleeveless and dipped into a deep V at the neck. Mark's position two stairs above her provided a clear shot into the V.

And here he'd thought worrying about their imminent meeting with Hayes and van Deursen would keep him awake all night!

## Chapter 5

They picked up a brisk, twenty-knot wind soon after clearing Bassaterre's harbor the next morning.

When Taylor raised the sails, the *Island Breeze* quickly gathered speed. The bow wave was huge and noisy as the wind drove the sloop through the foaming sea. Scudding clouds played hide and seek with the sun, bathing Taylor with alternate blasts of heat and blessed shade. Squinting under her sun visor, she adjusted their course to account for the stiff wind. She had to time their arrival to coincide with the low tide that would make the *Sea Breeze* vulnerable to the reef shoals ringing van Deursen's island.

Her nerves tightened a little more with every slap of a wave against the hull. Mark, too, tensed as St. Kitts's lush green hills dwindled to a hazy smudge. His face grim, he tracked their course by GPS and navigational chart.

Tension had them both by the throat when they sighted the group of islands strung out like little black beads in the distance. Most were uninhabited. A few, like van Deursen's, belonged to private investors.

Peeling off his sunglasses, Mark squinted at the largest in the string through the binoculars Constable Benjamin had provided.

"There it is. I recognize that jagged cliff from the reconnaissance photos."

Taylor nodded. If van Deursen's security was as tight as reported, she'd bet someone had a pair of binoculars trained on them, as well.

Her pulse kicking into overdrive, she tacked into the wind. Her narrow gaze alternated between the wide, clear channel at the tip of the island and the undulating lines of foamy white that marked the reef. As the *Island Breeze* plowed forward, its onboard sonar warning system began to ping.

She and Mark had talked about what would happen when they hit. Together, they'd rehearsed every move. Still, Taylor's heart began to thump as he eased the tiller a few degrees to starboard.

"We've got to make this look real," she warned. "Like we're bungling weekend sailors who realize too late they've run into trouble."

The sonar's ping rose to a shrill beep. Foaming waves crashed over the bow. Taylor curled her toes inside the canvas shoe containing her communications device and rapped out an order.

"Prepare to come about!"

Leaping forward, she secured a new jib sheet and uncleated the old. Tikal couldn't figure out what was happening but picked up on the sudden spike of tension. His short, excited barks punctuated the shout Taylor threw over her shoulder.

"Hard about! Now!"

Mark shoved the tiller, and the bow passed through the wind. When the boom began to swing, Taylor glanced across the bow and saw the sawtooth coral ridges rushing at the *Island Breeze* like open jaws.

"We're going to hit," she yelled. "Grab Tikal and brace yourself!"

Wrapping his right arm around the tiller, Mark hooked his left around the barking dog.

The sloop struck hard, slamming into the reef with a sickening crunch that almost threw Taylor over the side. She hung on, and for a breathless moment worried the keel might actually plow a path through the coral.

Then the deep V of the hull scraped, screeched and ripped wide-open. Mouthing a fervent apology to the mortally wounded sloop, Taylor scrambled for the deck well.

"Put on your life vest and inflate the raft," she yelled to Mark. "I'll send out a mayday."

The sloop had already begun to list. Pumping pure adrenaline, Taylor grabbed a life jacket and ducked through the hatch. Once in the galley she had to brace a hand against the tilting bulkhead while tuning the VHF radio to the channel reserved for hailing and distress signals.

"Mayday, mayday, mayday! This is the *Island Breeze,* out of Basseterre, St. Kitts."

Satellite imagery had shown that van Deursen maintained a multimillion dollar yacht and a small fleet of pleasure craft at his private marina. With such a large investment at stake, his people would keep an ear tuned for marine bulletins or weather alerts. Taylor knew they'd also pick up on distress signals that overrode normal frequencies.

Her heart pounding, she gave their present co-ordinates and the nature of their emergency. "We've struck a reef and ripped a hole in our hull. We're taking on water, fast. We have two souls aboard. I'm Taylor Chase. With me is Dr. Mark Wolfson, from Princeton University. We're preparing to abandon ship. Does anyone read me? Over."

Nothing but static crackled through the radio. If anyone on the island had heard the distress call, they weren't responding. Taylor waited a few moments and pressed the send button again.

"Mayday, mayday, mayday! This is the *Island Breeze,* out of Basseterre. We have two souls aboard, three counting our dog. Mark Wolfson, Taylor Chase and… Uh-oh! I've got water lapping at my ankles. We're abandoning ship. Over and out."

The initial phase of their scheme for accessing van Deursen's private island proceeded precisely according to plan. They'd struck the reef. The sloop was going down. They'd broadcast the distress call.

It was when they hit the water that things went to hell, fast.

Taylor and Mark heaved the inflatable raft over the side and dived in. Tikal leaped in beside them. They scrambled into the raft, had paddles in hand and were starting for shore when a monster wave came rushing toward them.

The rushing water lifted the crippled *Breeze* a good three or four feet, only to send her smashing down again. The sloop's fiberglass hull cracked like a peanut shell.

The same giant wave that sent the sloop to a watery grave tried to do the same to the rubber raft. The dinghy clung to the curl for ten, maybe fifteen yards before tipping at a steep angle. Taylor flattened herself against the side. Mark grabbed a wildly scrabbling Tikal.

Man and dog fell sideways, tipping the raft even further. When Taylor looked up, all she could see was the wall of water about to thunder down on them.

Mark tumbled through an angry green vortex for what felt like a lifetime before his life vest and strenuous kicking propelled him to the surface.

Riding the swells, he blinked seawater out of his eyes and spun in a circle.

Tikal had already popped up some distance away and was dog-paddling furiously toward the upended raft. Taylor... Christ! Where was Taylor?

Mark did another one-eighty. Still no sign of her. Fear slicing through him, he unclipped his vest, yanked it off and jackknifed. Enough sunlight filtered through the sea's surface for him to penetrate the murky green depths. He spotted a school of yellowjack, debris from the *Island Breeze,* the dark curve of an eel. But no Taylor.

His lungs bursting, he shot to the surface, sucked in a breath and dove again. His mind churned as furiously as his arms and legs.

Taylor had clipped on a life vest. It should have brought her up. Unless she'd snagged on the reef.

The coral ridge thrust up spiky arms fifty yards away. Fighting the current, Mark scissor-kicked through more swirling debris.

*Where are you? Taylor! Open the gate! Let me in! Where...?*

From the corner of one eye he caught a shadow of movement. Twisting, he spotted a pair of legs thrashing beneath the rubber life raft.

Relief speared through him, but lasted only until he grasped her predicament. The wave must have upended the raft and dropped it right on top of her. She couldn't get enough leverage to lift the thing and wiggle out from under its smothering weight.

Mark had started for her when another shadow glided into his field of vision. It swam toward him slowly, gracefully, with lethal intent.

With a jolt to his heart, he watched the shark approach. While his eyes cataloged the two dorsal fins, the pointed snout and spotted torso, his mind registered the relevant data.

Genus, *carcharias taurus. Carcharias* from the Greek, referring to its sharp, jagged teeth. *Taurus* from the Roman for bull, based on its stocky body. Family name, *Odontaspidae,* again from the Greek *odon,* or teeth. Common name, the Gray Nurse for its ability to "nurse" or round up small fish into a tight school for feeding.

Small fish. The Gray Nurse fed on small fish. Not large, dangling hunks of bait. Normally.

*Beat it, pal. I've got more urgent matters to attend to right now than you.*

It glided closer, its black eyes unblinking.

*Scram!*

The shark seemed to pause, then gave a silent flick of its tail and swam off. Mark didn't wait to see it disappear into the murky green. He was already kicking his way to Taylor. Her struggles had slowed, he saw with another jab of pure panic.

They'd ceased completely by the time he'd heaved the rubber dinghy up and heaved it over onto its right side. Taylor's life vest brought her to the surface. She floated there, facedown, until Mark manhandled her into the raft. Shoving Tikal in beside her, he lurched over the side.

His hands shook as he flipped Taylor over and tilted her head back. Her skin felt warm and slick, but when he bent to listen for sounds of breathing he couldn't hear anything but the hammering of his own heart. Swallowing a curse, he pinched her nose and gave her two quick breaths.

Nothing.

Mark unclipped her life jacket and rose up on his knees. The rubber dinghy shifted under his weight, making it impossible to maintain a steady rhythm as he leaned on her chest.

Fifteen one, fifteen two, fifteen three…

"Come on, Taylor! Breathe!"

Fifteen four, fifteen five…

What did the new guidelines say? Fifteen compressions before ventilation?

Mark insisted everyone at the lab receive CPR refresher training annually, himself included. But practicing on a dummy didn't come anywhere close to the terrifying reality of trying to pump air into Taylor's lungs.

Fifteen ten, fifteen eleven, fifteen…

Sweat mixed with the seawater streaming down his face and torso. Gulping in a deep breath, he pinched her nose again. He bent, covered her mouth and felt her twitch.

Her eyes flew open. She stared at him in dazed surprise for a second before her glance shifted to the dog who'd nosed his way in. Then her chest heaved, and he tipped her onto her side.

Seawater gushed out of her lungs. Gasping, she flopped onto her back again.

"Wh… What happened?"

"The dinghy came down on top of you. Took me a few minutes to find you."

More like a millennium. Mark wouldn't wipe out the memory of that agonizing search anytime soon. Taylor, either, judging by the way her fingers shook when she brushed them across her lips. Beneath wet, spiky lashes, her eyes telegraphed a question.

"You weren't breathing when I hauled you into the raft. I had to administer CPR."

"Oh. Uh, thanks."

"You're welcome."

No point in telling her about the Gray Nurse, he decided. She had enough to handle right now without knowing she could have become chum. He knelt beside her, waiting until she'd lost most of the green around her gills.

"Feel strong enough to sit up?"

Taylor's gratitude gave way to a flush of embarrassment. This was the second time she'd blacked out around him. If Wolfson hadn't nursed doubts about her ability to function in a potentially dangerous situation before, he *had* to be questioning it now.

"Thanks again. I'm okay now."

Her shoes had survived the immersion and frantic kicking, she saw with relief. The wet canvas squished as she got her feet under her and helped Mark retrieve the paddles. Thankfully thin safety lines had kept the oars from floating away.

They aimed for a narrow strip of beach at the

base of a hill covered with verdant green. As they paddled closer, Mark spotted gleaming white columns crowning the hilltop.

"There's the pool cabana Jack Bailey saw. And here's our welcoming committee."

Taylor squinted through the heat waves at the launch that rounded the island's north point. Two men stood in the deck well, another operated the controls. All three, she noted, wore black T-shirts, camouflage-type pants and sidearms.

A growl from just over her shoulder prompted a quick warning. "You'd better restrain Tikal. These guys don't look like real pet lovers."

Mark's silent communication quieted the animal but didn't dull his combative instincts. He stood braced on his forepaws behind Taylor, bathing her in dog breath and quivering antipathy.

"All right, team," she muttered under her breath. "It's showtime."

Raising her paddle, she waved it over her head. She didn't have to dig too deep to fake a joyous relief at their supposed rescue.

"Hey! Over here!"

Pretty stupid, considering the launch was headed right for the raft. Taylor shrugged the

thought aside and stuck to her role as one half of
the inept pair who'd just sailed their boat into a
reef. Still waving, she waited for them to cut the
engine and drift closer.

"Thank God you heard our distress call! I
wasn't sure anyone had picked it up. Tikal! Hush!"

With rumbles rolling around in the furry chest
just inches from her ear, Taylor grabbed the line
one of the men tossed. Mark caught the other but
held off hauling the raft any closer to the motor-
boat.

"What's with the guns?" he asked, getting into
his role. "Have we strayed into a military zone or
something?"

"We are security guards," one of the three
answered in the British-accented, Caribbean-
flavored English of St. Kitts. "You have strayed
into private waters. We will return you to Basseterre so you may report your unfortunate accident
to the proper authorities."

"Thanks, but we can't leave until we see what
we can salvage from our boat."

"I'm afraid we must insist."

"You don't understand," Taylor put in. "This is
Dr. Mark Wolfson. He's a professor at Princeton

University, in the States. I'm his assistant. We collected some important data on the behavior of marine mammals during our sail. We have to try to retrieve what we can."

"I'm sorry, sir, but my comrades and I have our orders. We will take you to Basseterre."

"You have a radio," Mark said with a touch of impatience. "Let me speak to your superior."

"Our superior is the one who dispatched us when your boat struck the reef."

"Get him on the radio."

The guard's eyes narrowed but he nodded to the man at the controls. "Do as he requests."

*So much for your scheme to get us on the island!*

When Mark's sarcastic voice reverberated in her head, Taylor almost jumped out of her skin.

*Don't DO that!*

*Then close the damned gate.*

*I didn't know I'd opened it.*

*Must have happened when we hit the reef.*

Taylor was trying to summon an image of her grandparents' shed when the man at the controls of the launch clipped the radio mic into place and addressed his companions.

"We have a change in orders. Yardley says to bring them to the dock."

The muscle-type who'd insisted they'd have to return to Basseterre accepted the change of orders with a shrug.

"Very well. Come aboard, if you please. We'll tow your raft."

Taylor and Mark made the transfer with the assistance of the two guards. Tikal leaped aboard in one bound. Once the raft was secure, the operator gunned the engine and made a wide sweep. A few moments later the launch rounded the point.

Taylor recorded their approach with the precision of a digital camera. They were headed for a dock that jutted out from what looked like a sheer precipice. A boathouse extended over one side of the dock, with hoists ready to raise the launch and tuck it away. Slips housed watercraft that ranged from wave runners to ski boats.

At the end of the pier was a helipad. A sleek Bell JetRanger III sat on the pad, painted a distinctive red and black. The prominent DvD logo on its fuselage identified it as part of Diederik van Deursen's private fleet.

A flutter of movement drew Taylor's eyes to the

wooden stairs that zigzagged up the cliff face. Or rather, to the figures descending the stairs. One was in uniform. The captain of the guard, Taylor guessed. The other wore white slacks and a loose-fitting Panama shirt. Even at this distance she recognized Diederik van Deursen from the photos Intel had gathered.

Squinting, Taylor watched the billionaire descend the stairs with languid grace. He'd appeared bigger in the photos. More charismatic. The tropical sun and this suffocating heat must have sapped his energy.

Or maybe the man was sick.

Eyes narrowing, she studied him more closely. He seemed pale, but that could be a reflection of the glare from the sea. He seemed thinner, too. Damn! Why hadn't she requested a health assessment.

*Van Deursen's a recluse. He'd guard his medical records more closely than his finances.*

Taylor whipped her head around and skewered Mark with a rapier look.

*Stop interfering with my thinking! I need to concentrate.*

*Then close the damned portal.*

Jaw locked, she squeezed her eyes shut and summoned the image of a dilapidated shed.

*Did you hear the gate bang, Wolfson? I'm locking it. Right now.*

Just to be safe, she hummed under her breath for the rest of the way in. She didn't break off the nasal tune until the launch had nosed up to the dock and been secured.

The guard who'd descended the stairs with van Deursen reached out a hand to assist Taylor onto the pier. Mark stepped up on his own, as did Tikal.

"Ms. Chase. Dr. Wolfson. My name is Diederik van Deursen."

The man's handshake was as limp and unenergetic as his movements.

"I apologize if my employees appeared overzealous in their determination to return you to Basseterre. I'm rather protective of my privacy."

"So we gathered."

"However, I believe you may be acquainted with a guest of mine. Dr. Oscar Hayes?"

Mark's look of blank surprise would have qualified him for an Emmy. "Oscar's here?"

"Indeed he is. He became quite excited when he heard you were aboard the capsized boat."

Van Deursen's gaze lingered on Mark. Taylor held her breath and prayed the billionaire had taken the bait.

"Oscar told me your work may well complement his own efforts. As they are of special interest to me, I'm very curious about what you do. I hope you'll permit me to offer you and your lovely assistant my hospitality while you recover from your accident."

*We're in!*

Taylor waited a beat after her gleeful mental exclamation. When Mark didn't reply in kind, she let out a relieved breath and followed her host along the dock. Instead of taking the stairs, however, he gestured to a set of tracks concealed by the greenery.

"The stairs are quite steep, so I had a cog lift installed for the comfort and convenience of my guests. After you, Ms. Chase."

# Chapter 6

Taylor's profession had taken her to a number of exotic spots around the world. Whenever possible, she'd toured the local area and had eaten or downed a drink in everything from dirt-floored huts to fairy-tale castles perched high in the Bavarian Alps. But she'd *never* seen anything as sumptuous as Diederik van Deursen's Caribbean hideaway.

"Welcome to my home."

Smiling, their slim, elegant host ushered them along a flagstone walk bordered with marble statuary and shrubs in a hundred different shades of green. Flowers were massed amid the shrubs, thick and almost overpowering in their fragrance. Pink and purple hibiscus, swaying red oleander, bird of paradise and a dozen more varieties Taylor couldn't name. Glossy elephant ear vines snaked around the trunks of towering palms and climbed almost to the treetops. A stream trickled through pebbled pools, adding its water song to the rise and fall of the waves below.

Van Deursen's security system was both state-of-the-art and conspicuously visible. Taylor noted spots and passive sensors placed at strategic angles and heights along the walkway. Infrared and motion operated, obviously. She'd bet a big chunk of next month's pay there were redundant and more powerful devices hidden among the lush greenery.

The soothing trickle of the stream gained in volume and ended abruptly in a splashing waterfall. No, not a waterfall, Taylor corrected as she followed van Deursen up a short flight of flagstone steps. A spill from a free-flowing, multitiered swimming pool that, at its bottom level, appeared to fall straight into the sea. Behind the pool stood the columns of the Greek temple Jack Bailey had described.

"Ah, there's my wife."

Bailey had certainly pegged the champagne-blonde stretched out in a chase lounge inside the temple/cabana. She *was* a looker. From a man's perspective, anyway. Long-legged and so lavishly endowed that her bikini top was completely super-fluous, she lay with one knee bent and her face raised to the sun.

"Darling," van Deursen called, "come and meet our unexpected guests."

She popped upright and slid her sunglasses down her nose to view the newcomers. "Guests?"

Shoving her feet into high-heeled sandals, she hurried across the terrace. The pungent tang of sunscreen wafted from her glistening torso when she joined her husband. With the added height of her sandals and teased hair, she towered a good three or four inches above van Deursen.

He didn't seem to mind. Sliding an arm around her oil-slicked waist, he made the introductions. "Beverly, this is Dr. Mark Wolfson and his companion, Taylor Chase."

The sunglasses tipped downward again. "What'd y'all do? Swim ashore?"

"Almost." Manfully Mark kept his gaze above

bikini level. "We hit a reef and had to abandon our sailboat. Your husband came to our rescue."

"That's my Diederik," she cooed, dropping a kiss on the top of her spouse's head. "He's a champ at chargin' to the rescue."

Almost gagging on the saccharine overdose, Taylor matched both the face and the Texas drawl to the dossier Intel had compiled on Beverly Johnson van Deursen.

Twenty-three. Born in a one-stop-sign town about twenty miles south of San Antonio. Dropped out of high school to run off with a trucker who beat her to a pulp before dumping her in Gallup, New Mexico. She subsequently worked her way to California via a variety of jobs that included migrant crop picker, short-order cook and parking lot attendant. Met forty-three-year-old Diederik van Deursen last year during one of his rare trips to the States, when she parked his rented BMW at L.A.'s latest in-spot.

The match between the tall, voluptuous Texan and the reclusive billionaire would have triggered an Anna Nicole Smith-style frenzy in the media if van Deursen wasn't such a fanatic about his privacy. He'd whisked his bride off to his tropical paradise before the media had caught a whiff of their romance. She'd remained here ever since.

"And who's this?" she asked, eyeing the animal at Mark's side.

"This is Tikal."

"Hey, fella. Aren't you just the sweetest thing?"

To Taylor's astonishment, the wet, shaggy creature submitted to the indignity of having his ear tugged without a single curl of his gums. Evidently Tikal wasn't any more immune to top-heavy Texans than van Deursen.

Giving his ear another playful pull, Beverly stood and hooked her arm through Taylor's. "You just come with me, Mz. Chase, and we'll get you out of those wet clothes."

"Please, call me Taylor."

"I'll do that. 'N you call me Bev. Just come along with me now. I've got closets full of clothes. I'm sure we'll find something to fit you."

Taylor seriously doubted that. She and her hostess were about the same height but Beverly boasted far more generous curves.

She wasn't about to pass up the chance to sneak a peek at the van Deursen's private quarters, however. With a nod to Mark, she accompanied the blonde up another short flight of steps.

The ascent brought them to the top tier of the pool, which lapped right up to the residence surrounding it on three sides. Pillared porticos connected separate wings to the main unit, while floor-to-ceiling sliding glass panels left each section open to the tropical breeze.

"That there's the living and dining room."

Beverly gestured to the two-story central structure. Taylor caught a glimpse of a massive chandelier suspended above a table the size of a hockey rink. Rattan-backed dining chairs were lined up on either side of the table like skaters in a face-off.

"This here's my wing." Beverly guided Taylor to a set of open glass doors. "Mine and Diederik's. After I get you outfitted, we'll put you 'n... What was your hunky friend's name again?"

"Mark. Mark Wolfson."

"Funny name but it fits. Him and his dog both look like they've got some wild in them."

The same thought had occurred to Taylor. More than once, as a matter of fact.

"We'll put you 'n Mark in the guest wing."

"I hope we're not inconveniencing you or your other guests."

As probes went, that one was about as subtle as a cattle prod but Taylor wasn't too worried about finessing information out of her hostess. If Beverly van Deursen's microdot bikini was any indication, she didn't go in for subtle or under-stated.

"Inconveniencing us? Lord, no! The guest wing's got four bedrooms, five bathrooms, its own kitchen, a private spa and a home theater. Y'all won't need to cook, though. Diederik's chef takes care of that. And you'll have the spa to yourself. Our other guest don't…" She stopped, made a face, and corrected herself. "Oscar *doesn't* work out none."

This was almost too easy.

"Oscar?"

"Oscar Hayes."

"Oh, right. Your husband mentioned he was here. Is he vacationing with you?"

"Sorta, although as much time as he spends in the lab, you'd think he was on the payroll. Hey, didn't Diederik say your guy is a doc, too?"

"He holds Ph.D.'s in zoology and behavioral science."

"Well, ain't that a kick!"

Since no response appeared to be expected, Taylor merely smiled and followed Beverly into her sumptuous suite. It was done in an elegant South Seas decor. The pool flowed right into the sitting room to make it a sort of indoor/outdoor spa complete with sunken marble hot tub, wet bar and stereo surround sound.

The room beyond boasted a net-draped bed on a raised dais and more marble. Ceiling fans stirred air that was mechanically cooled despite the wide-open glass doors.

"Okay, let's see what we got here."

When Beverly flung open a set of louvered doors, Taylor's jaw almost hit her sternum. The walk-in closet was larger than her D.C. condo. It was also the equivalent of an Aladdin's Cave for any female who'd ever lusted for a Versace gown or a pair of Giuseppe Zanotti shoes.

"Good Lord," she muttered, awestruck.

"I know." Beverly gave a delighted giggle. "Diederik insisted on buying me a... What'dya call it? A tru...?"

"Trousseau?"

"Yeah, that's it. God knows when I'll get to

wear this fancy stuff. Diederik ain't one to… Oops."

Rolling her eyes, the blonde clamped a hand over her mouth. When she lowered it again, embarrassment stained her cheeks a bright pink.

"There I go again. My husband's been after me to shed some of my hick talk. I'm tryin'. I'm really tryin'. Kinda hard to kick a lifetime of he ain'ts and he don'ts, though."

Was the woman for real? Taylor couldn't decide. Every surface indication suggested this gregarious, seemingly guileless female couldn't be involved in the abduction of Oscar Hayes, much less the sale of genetically engineered body parts on the black market. Until Taylor got a fix on Hayes's activities, however, she would take nothing as a given. Including Ms. Beverly van Deursen.

"Let's find you something cool 'n comfy."

Bypassing several racks of gowns and cocktail dresses, Beverly aimed for a section of casual wear any resort boutique manager would have killed for.

"Here, this'll fit you." She pulled a silky caftan in a riot of reds off its hanger and reached for a sleeveless silk tunic in dark cobalt. "And this. And these drawstring gauze slacks. And…"

"Whoa! This is more than enough to keep me covered until my shorts and tank top dry."

"You'd better stock up. No telling how long it will take the boys to fix your boat."

"I, er, don't think it's fixable. It broke apart on the reef."

"No shit?" A happy smile lit her face. "Too bad for you but good for me. I've been itchin' for another woman to gab with. Mz. White and Thérèse are okay, but Diederik don't…*doesn't*… like me to bend elbows with the help."

Yanking open a drawer, she extracted a froth of black silk and lace. "Here's a nightie. Now for some undies."

The lace thong Beverly pulled out contained even less fabric than her bikini bottom. It was Bev's size, but the elastic waistband would keep the thing from sliding right off Taylor. The same couldn't be said of the thongs' matching double-D bra.

"Dang! Looks like this was made for a pregnant cow. Sure won't do for you." Shaking her head, Beverly tossed the bra back in the drawer. "You might have to go without."

"I'm okay," Taylor said hastily.

"Suit yourself. Here's a pair of sandals." She added wedgies to the pile and tapped a coral-tipped nail against her chin. "What'd we forget?"

"Maybe some shampoo? I need to wash the salt and seaweed out of my hair."

"There's shampoo 'n lotion 'n all in the guest baths. We'll put you in the Governor's suite. I'll show you where it is 'n leave you to clean up. We usually have cocktails on the terrace at six. Wander on out before then if you want. I'll be hangin' somewhere."

As they entered the guest wing, Taylor picked up a faint cherry fragrance lingering in the hall.

"Is that a cigar I smell?"

"Pipe," Bev replied. "Oscar always has one lit when he's outside. He puts it out before he comes inside, but the smoke follows him a little. You won't notice it none in your rooms," she promised, throwing open the door to the Governor's suite. "Here you are. I'll leave you to get settled. Just pick up the phone and ask for housekeeping if you need anything."

"Thanks, I will."

The lavishly decorated rooms oozed British colonial ambiance. The upholstery was rich gold, splashed with touches of royal-blue. The dark mahogany furniture featured intricate carving.

A net-draped, king-size bed caught her attention, but Taylor didn't allow herself to dwell on the fact that she and Mark would share it. This was a mission, an op. She'd slept in muddy ditches before and shared body heat with half-frozen team members during a trek across the Tundra. And last night, on the *Island Breeze,* she and Mark had worked out satisfactory sleeping arrangements. They'd do the same tonight.

With that thought fixed firmly in her head, she unlatched the louvered doors that opened onto the pool and drank in the throat-catching view of the sea beyond.

She itched to share Beverly's artless disclosures with Mark but needed to sweep the rooms first. Although she hadn't spotted any visible surveillance cameras in the guest suites, Taylor would bet the rooms were bugged. Anyone as obsessed with security and privacy as van Deursen would want to be sure his guests were protected, if not closely observed.

Heading into the lavish bath, she unlaced her wet deck shoes. Casually, so casually, she made a pretense of squeezing the water out of them into the Olympic-size bathtub. In the process, she peeled back the insole and pressed the star key on the concealed phone for two seconds to let Sergeant Powell know that she had the situation under control.

She hoped!

That done, she activated the electronic sweep. Sure enough, the indicator glowed a discreet red. She and Mark would have to watch every word. Sliding the phone back into place, she set the shoe aside and turned the taps to full-blast. Using the little silver scoop provided by her thoughtful hosts, she shoveled fragrant bath salts into the tub. Within seconds the heavy, heady scent of gardenias rose with the steam.

The luxurious bathroom also included thin cotton robes, freshly ironed and folded neatly in wicker holders. Taylor snagged one of the robes and laid it on the edge of the tub before stripping off her wet clothes.

If the bathroom did have hidden cameras, she was providing some watcher a peep show. Hope he enjoyed it. Sinking into the steamy bubbles, she forced the tension from her neck and shoulders. She couldn't force it from her mind.

Where was Mark? What was taking him so long?

Antsy and wanting to compare notes, she wondered if the portal technique worked in short bursts. Could she open the gate, send him a quick salvo, and slam it shut again?

Deciding to give it a try, she closed her eyes and visualized her grandparents' shed.

Unlock the gate. Check.

Open it. Check.

Summon the percipient.

*Yo! Wolfson!*

She waited, feeling uneasy and a little ridiculous at the same time, while an image formed in her head. No doubt about it. She'd summoned the right man. Hair dripping, skin drawn tight across his cheeks, Mark leaned over her.

When his mouth came down on hers, Taylor realized she was reliving those moments after he'd dragged her from the sea. She could feel his hands anchoring her head as he forced air into her lungs, taste him all wet and salty and hot.

She sank lower in the tub as the scene blurred around the edges. The texture and color of Mark's image shifted. She could still feel his lips crushing hers, still hear the thunder of his heart. Or was that hers booming like a field artillery piece?

Her knees bent. She eased down farther, until the water licked at her chin. Sensations seemed to come at her from all directions. Dark. Sensual. Intense.

The violent spasm low in her belly brought her sloshing upright. Whoa! Enough of that.

She gave herself a swift mental kick for inviting the erotic invasion and lathered up. She was rinsing off a head full of shampoo when something cold and wet poked her in the right breast.

"Dammit, Tikal!"

The dog plopped down on his haunches beside the tub. Taylor could swear his lips curled back in the equivalent of a canine grin.

The man who leaned against the doorjamb also wore a grin. His was far easier to read. Broad and unrepentant, it told Taylor he'd been there long enough for an eyeful.

"You called?"

She started to tell him to be careful what he said but swallowed the caution just in time. Had she left the gate open? Could she communicate a warning that way?

Mark stiffened. His eyes lost their glint.

*Warning about what?*

*The room. It's bugged.*

*We're being watched?*

*Watched, or listened to.*

Slicking back her wet hair, Taylor reverted to verbal communication for the benefit of any interested observers.

"Where were you just now?"

"In the van Deursens's study. I used their phone to contact the marina in St. Kitts to report the accident."

"Uh-oh. Bet they weren't real happy to hear we lost the *Island Breeze.*"

"All I can say is it's a good thing we opted for full insurance coverage when we rented the sloop."

"Did you talk to van Deursen about trying to salvage some of our research materials? The laptop is a goner, of course, but I sealed our handwritten notes in a waterproof container with the ship's log."

"Van Deursen says his men maintain a full complement of scuba gear at the marina. He'll send some divers down to see what they can find."

Still playing to any unseen recording devices, Taylor pursed her lips. "Don't you think this is a little weird?"

Mark didn't alter his relaxed stance, but a wariness entered his eyes. *What are you doing, Chase?*

*Just follow my lead.*

"Weird how?"

"The armed guards," she said with a vague gesture toward the open glass doors. "The way they tried to turn us away at first. It's an unwritten law of the sea that you render aid to someone in distress."

"Van Deursen explained that. Paparazzi have resorted to all sorts of stratagems to gain access to this island. His men have standing instructions to escort uninvited visitors back to Basseterre."

"That's another thing. Who is this guy? Why does he go to such lengths to keep the world out?"

"Look around you. It's obvious he's got a few bucks in the bank. I would guess he wants to make sure he and his family don't become targets."

When she let the conversation trail off, Mark shoved away from the doorjamb and hooked his thumb toward the well-stocked bar in the outer room. "You want a drink?"

"Beverly said something about drinks on the terrace at six."

"That's a good three hours from now. I need to wash down all the salt water I swallowed."

"Make it fairly innocuous and I'll join you."

"I think I saw some champagne."

"That'll do."

Grabbing a towel, she dried off quickly and pulled on the freshly ironed robe.

The borrowed thong panties took some getting used to. Squirming, she adjusted the thong and finger-combed her hair before joining Mark and Tikal in the living room of their suite. The dog was stretched out on the cool tiles by the door. Mark was tipping champagne into crystal flutes.

"Do you believe all this?" she asked with a nod toward the flat-screen plasma TV and its high-tech sound system. "Maybe we should forget about trying to make it to the other islands and see if the van Deursens will let us camp out here a few weeks."

"Maybe we should." Handing her a flute, he followed her cue. "It would sure beat sharing a cramped cabin imbued with the odor of wet fur."

Taylor held up her glass. "Shall we drink to the *Island Breeze?*"

"That, and our close call this afternoon." His flute clinked against hers. *That's about as intimate as I want to get with a* carcharias taurus.

*A what?*

*I'll tell you about it later.*

Mark tipped his glass to his lips and tried to rein in his galloping nerves. He'd uncorked the champagne in deference to Taylor's request to keep it light, but he sure could have used a shot of something stronger. This light fizz didn't do anything to ease the tension cording the tendons in his neck.

The cat and mouse game with van Deursen was bad enough. He'd had to watch every word while they were in the study. This business about listening devices and surveillance cameras only made it worse.

Not that he could relax, even without the bugs. All it took was one glimpse of the thin cotton clinging to Taylor's still damp body to tie him into knots no sailor could ever untangle. He downed another swallow of champagne, fiercely conscious of the dark aureoles and nipples pushing against the cotton.

Taylor's head came up. Her green eyes flashed a warning. *Careful, Wolfson.*

*You said we're being watched. We need to convince them we're who we say we are.*

Removing the crystal flute from her hand, he set it aside with his and hooked an arm around her waist.

*Hang on a minute, bub!*

"I almost lost you this afternoon, Taylor. I don't think I knew until that moment how much you mean to me."

*No?* Derision mixed with the back-off signals pulsing from her in waves. *You gave me a pretty good indication eight years ago.*

"I don't want to lose you again."

He pulled her closer, his smile tender and loving.

*I'll get you for this, Wolfson.*

*Shut up and kiss me.*

# Chapter 7

Taylor shut up and kissed him.

She didn't want to. Well, maybe she did, a little, but only in the line of duty. Or maybe she wanted to test the waters, see if Wolfson could deliver the same punch in the flesh as he did in her subconscious a few moments ago. Whatever the motivation, she knew she had to make the kiss look good to any unseen watchers.

Determined to give a credible performance, she looped her arms around his neck and locked her mouth on his. She could taste the salt on his lips, as she had in the tub, and the heat. God, the heat! It transferred to her skin when he tightened his arm and pressed her closer, igniting little sparks at every contact point.

Yielding to the sizzle, she opened her mouth. Her tongue scraped his teeth. Her palms played over his back and shoulders. Beneath his torn shirt his muscles bunched into tight coils.

Mark, too, gave an exceptional performance. *Extremely* exceptional. Widening his stance, he brought her into the cradle of his hips. So near, Taylor felt him harden against her belly. Her stomach rolled, swift and tight, in answer to the bulge behind the zipper of his still damp shorts.

A rumble emanating from deep in Tikal's chest was the first indication they had company. The tread of footsteps on the terrace outside the open glass doors confirmed it.

Smothering a curse, Mark raised his head. Taylor took a fleeting satisfaction in the heat staining his cheeks before craning around to see who'd joined them. Her already skittering pulse got another jolt when she spotted the man who came to a halt in the doorway.

"I'm so sorry!"

There he was, the scientist she'd been sent to find. Only *he'd* found them.

"I didn't mean to intrude," Hayes apologized with only a trace of the accent he'd brought with him when he'd emigrated from Germany as a young boy.

"Hello, Oscar. You're not intruding."

Taylor used the shield of Mark's back to belt the thin cotton robe more securely. While she made sure she was covered, he crossed the room.

"I couldn't believe it when van Deursen told me you were here on his island, working on a special project for him."

The two men clasped hands, affording Taylor the opportunity to compare the geneticist to the photos in the dossier she'd studied. The frizzy gray hair was the same. So were the liver spots dotting his face and the black-framed glasses with their bottle-thick lenses. He'd acquired another network of wrinkles to go with the age spots, though, and his shoulders slumped tiredly under his white lab coat.

"I, too, was amazed when I heard you were aboard the boat sending distress signals," Hayes said. His gaze swept over Mark's torn shirt and shorts. "You weren't injured when it went down, I hope."

"I'm fine. Taylor swallowed half the Caribbean, though." Turning, Mark invited her to join him. "Come meet a friend and former colleague."

The scientist brought the faint odor of sweet, cherry tobacco in with him. Taylor recognized the scent as she moved to Mark's side.

"This is Dr. Oscar Hayes," he said. "We coauthored a paper on the nesting habits of leatherback turtles some years back."

"I know. I read it before I came to work for you." She returned Hayes's handshake with a smile. "I was intrigued by your findings that genetic differences in successive generations of the same family affect how deeply the leatherbacks burrow into the sand to build their nests."

The scientist regarded her with surprise and dawning respect. "May I say it sounds as though Mark has found an associate as intelligent as she is lovely?"

"You may indeed, sir."

Hayes's gaze shifted to the dog watching their every move. "And who is this?"

"This is Tikal."

"He has wolf in him, does he not? *Canis lupus pambasileus,* I would guess."

"*Canis lupus tundrarum*," Mark corrected.

"Ah, yes. Of course. The two subspecies are similar in size and habitat, but the Tundra wolves have more silver in their fur."

Hayes didn't succeed in establishing the same instant rapport Beverly van Deursen had. Although he held out a hand, Tikal remained where he was, ears pricked forward, eyes narrowed.

"We just opened a bottle of champagne to toast our rescue," Mark said to end the brief stand-off. "Would you like to join us in a glass?"

"No, no, I cannot."

Straightening, Hayes thrust his hands in the pockets of his lab coat. His glance darted to a spot over Taylor's shoulder. It came back almost immediately, but the quick, furtive look confirmed he knew they were being watched or recorded.

"I must return to the lab," Hayes said. "I merely came to invite you to visit the facilities and view my latest work. You, too, Ms. Chase. When you are rested and recovered from your ordeal."

She was fully recovered—or had been until Mark's kiss knocked her off-kilter again—but let him answer for both of them.

"I'd be very interested in seeing what you're

working on these days, Oscar. Give me a few minutes to clean up and change into the clothes I borrowed from one of van Deursen's men."

"Take as long as you like. Just pick up the phone and dial three-three-seven when you're ready. Someone will escort you." He turned to Taylor and bowed a little with Old World charm. "A pleasure to meet you, Ms. Chase. I look forward to furthering our acquaintance."

Her gaze thoughtful, she watched as he retreated through the open terrace doors. Would it really be this easy? Would she and Mark get onto the island and into the lab, all within a few hours? Once there, would she learn whether Hayes had abandoned his ongoing projects in the States and secluded himself on this remote island voluntarily?

Her gut said no, that none of the key players she and Mark had encountered so far were what they seemed. The reclusive, almost effete billionaire, his buxom bride, the grandfatherly scientist with the tired eyes and sagging shoulders—they all came across as too friendly, too welcoming.

Too bad Mark couldn't get inside *their* heads. *They're not as receptive to my vibes as you are.* Oh, hell! She'd left the friggin' gate open.

Again. With a mental kick, she sent the door to her grandparents' shed careening on its rusty hinges.

Mark acknowledged the screech with a sardonic nod. "You get dressed, I'll grab a shower and we'll take Oscar up on his invitation."

The white drawstring pants Beverly had loaned her were cool and comfortable, but a little too sheer. Thankfully the sleeveless cobalt tunic reached below Taylor's hips and covered the patch of thong showing through the slacks.

The shower cut off just as she was lacing the ties to her still damp boat shoes. Training and habit dictated she keep her concealed communications device with her at all times. The soggy canvas didn't do much for the designer slacks and top, but she'd use the built-in excuse that Beverly's three-inch platforms were a size too large.

"Ready?"

Buttoning a brightly colored tropical shirt, Mark exited the bathroom. Taylor itched to get him someplace they could compare notes without fear of being overheard or recorded, but that would have to wait. Nodding, she lifted the phone.

"What number did Dr. Hayes say to call?"

"Three-three-seven."

The male who answered spoke with the British-accented English of St. Kitts. "Regeneration Facility."

Taylor's fist tightened on the phone. Just what were they regenerating?

"This is Taylor Chase. Mark Wolfson and I spoke with Dr. Hayes a little while ago and he said to call this number when we were ready to visit your facility."

"Yes, Ms. Chase. Dr. Hayes told us to expect your call. I'll come straight away to fetch you."

When their escort arrived a scant few minutes later, Taylor realized she'd mistaken his accent. Sulim Rasjan's dark, liquid eyes and olive skin proclaimed his heritage even before he identified himself as a native of Mumbai.

India, the Netherlands, Germany, St. Kitts, the sovereign state of Texas—they were all represented on this tiny speck of an island. Diederik van Deursen operated a regular United Nations.

"It's a pleasure to meet you, Dr. Wolfson. Dr. Hayes had told me something of your work. If you and Ms. Chase will please to come with me…"

Signaling Tikal to stay, Mark put a hand to the

small of Taylor's back. The polite, possessive gesture was strictly for show, of course. No reason in hell for shivers to crawl up and down her spine.

His hand moved from her back to her elbow during the descent to the lower tier of the terrace. A golf cart waited for them at the edge of the flagstones. Handing Taylor into the front seat beside Rasjan, Mark took one of the side-facing rear benches.

The cart putt-putted around the sprawling residence and into another of the green tunnels that formed the main passageways of van Deursen's island. Once again Taylor breathed in the pungent mix of flowering hibiscus and dank, rotting vegetation.

The cart emerged from the tunnel into a flat expanse hacked out of the jungle. Directly ahead stood a cluster of white buildings surrounded by an electrified fence. Rolls of concertina wire topped the chain link, reminding Taylor all too forcefully of similar compounds in the heavy drug trafficking regions of Colombia.

She'd studied the satellite imagery of this particular compound. Seeing it up close and personal like this, however, brought her mission into dramatic focus. Interesting that Diederik van Deursen felt he had to protect whatever was going on behind the wire from prying eyes, even on his own private island.

The guard at the entrance to the compound hailed their escort by name, but the heavy gate didn't rattle open until Rasjan tilted his head to stare into a camera. An iris recognition scanner, Taylor guessed, in keeping with the latest generation surveillance equipment mounted at regular intervals around the compound.

Once cleared, Rasjan scooted around a windowless square-block building and parked at the entrance to another. "I don't know how much Dr. Hayes has told you of our work here," he said as he ushered them to the door.

"Nothing, actually."

"Ah, then I must not steal his thunder." His dark eyes glowed with unmistakable pride. "But you will be amazed, I think, to see what we have accomplished in the short time since Oscar has joined us on Eeuwigheid."

"Eh-oi-what?"

"Wig-heid. Please excuse me. I don't speak the language of the Netherlands very well and cannot wrap my tongue around the name Mr. van Deursen has given his island."

Taylor didn't speak Dutch at all and none of the maps she'd studied had labeled the island. Tucking the syllables away in the back of her mind, she stood to one side as Rasjan keyed the door.

The first thing that hit her when she stepped inside was the sterility of the reception area. Tiled floor, unadorned walls, severely tilted blinds—all in unrelieved, unrelenting white. Almost before she'd absorbed the complete lack of color, however, Taylor registered the faint, fishy smell emanating from somewhere behind the bars blocking the corridor that led off the reception area.

Her glance zinged to Mark. His expression remained neutral, but he had to have caught a whiff of it. Heparin, the naturally occurring anti-coagulant used to preserve organs prior to transplant.

"This is Ms. Chase and Dr. Wolfson, guests of Mr. van Deursen," Rasjan announced. "He and Dr. Hayes have cleared them into the facility."

Craning her neck, Taylor saw her face, then Mark's, flash onto the screen behind the counter.

They were frozen against an achingly blue sea, their hair wet and dripping. One of their rescuers must have clicked a hidden camera and beamed their pictures up to the control center before bringing them in.

She held her breath until the guard pressed a hidden release.

The bars glided up on silent tracks. The long hallway beckoned. To Taylor's intense disappointment, the doors leading off the corridor had no glass windows or inserts allowing a peek beyond their solid shield but the seaweedy scent intensified with every step.

Rasjan stopped at the second door from the last and slid his ID into a card slot. "We maintain a sterile environment," he warned. "Once inside, you must scrub and don surgical gowns, hoods, foot covers and masks before proceeding into the lab."

Anticipation had Taylor wound in such a tight coil she barely felt the scrape of the stiff-bristled scrub brush when she lathered her arms and hands. Her breath was hot behind her surgical mask as she shuffled through another door ahead of Mark.

She wasn't sure what she'd expected, but this chill, empty room wasn't it. There wasn't a test tube or petri dish in sight. Just a counter with a stainless steel sink at one end and a rack containing a row of clear plastic containers at the other. The odor of heparin was so strong she forced herself to breathe through her mouth.

"Mark. Ms. Chase." His voice muffled by his surgical mask, Oscar Hayes rounded the counter. "Welcome to the Regenerating Room."

Despite the icebox chill of the interior, sweat darkened the paper cap that corralled the scientist's frizzy hair. Mark had to note Hayes's nervous perspiration as well, but his reply reflected only academic curiosity.

"Exactly what are you regenerating, Oscar?"

"A liver. A pancreas. Two kidneys." Hayes gestured to the refrigerated unit. "A section of lower intestine. All from genetic material provided by a donor."

Mark's gaze sliced into the older man, as sharp as a scalpel. "A liver has the ability to regenerate. Kidneys, pancreatic material and intestines don't."

"They do," Hayes said, holding his eyes, "if you alter their DNA structure."

"Jesus, Oscar! I heard you were experimenting

with genetic engineering. Are you telling me you've broken the nucleic acid code?"

"Not completely. But I...we," he amended with a sideways glance at Rasjan, "are very close. Look here."

He led the way to the glass-fronted cabinet at the end of the counter. Its stainless steel shelves held two rows of oblong containers. Each appeared to be about twice the size of a shoebox.

These weren't ordinary shoeboxes, however. Tubes and wires fed into them from various sources, and each case came with its own data screen, cipher lock and temperature control. Skimming the screen, Taylor saw the contents were kept at forty degrees Fahrenheit.

"These are specially designed cryogenic containers," Hayes explained. "Let's show them BK-769.6, Sulim."

His assistant opened the cabinet and activated some unseen mechanism. A second later, one of the cases slid forward. Once exposed to the air in the lab, the clear plastic case fogged until Hayes ran a hand over it slowly, almost lovingly, to clear the mist.

"Diederik van Deursen hired a team of the world's leading engineers to design these incubators. Their polymer coating contains both heat and cold without transferring either. We can regulate the temperature inside to within plus or minus point zero five on a nanometer."

Hayes edged to the side, and Taylor spotted an oblong object floating in colorless liquid inside the container.

"This is living pancreatic material. It's regenerating itself."

Mark sucked in a sharp breath and bent in for a closer look.

"As you may be aware," Hayes continued slowly, "two researchers in Switzerland recently isolated the DNA sequence that governs molecular growth in the human pancreas."

Removing his glasses, the scientist polished them on a corner of his lab coat. Taylor got the distinct impression he was measuring every word. No surprise there, considering the implications of that small tissue sample.

"Using their work as a baseline, we extracted the growth DNA sequence from the cell of a diseased pancreas and replaced it with the DNA of a foreign donor."

"Foreign?" Mark echoed.

The bottle-thick glasses received another slow polish.

"The healthy sequence was extracted from a bovine."

The bovine part wasn't all that startling. Scientists had harvested organic material from cows—and pigs and rats—for decades.

Same with genetic modification. Critical drugs like insulin and the human growth hormone had been genetically engineered from other substances.

When you put the two together, however, things got dicey. Particularly if the intent was to transplant these genetically modified organs into human recipients.

Taylor couldn't take her eyes from the incubator. She knew the arguments, had read the pros and cons, understood the concern about populating the future with living organisms engineered to predetermined specifications.

Yet tissue like this could save countless lives, spare untold victims of accident or diseases the kind of agony her brother had endured—*if* and when Hayes received approval to test it on human subjects from the FDA or AMA or whoever governed such matters.

Her gaze locked on the living tissue inside the incubator, Taylor put the question to Dr. Hayes. "How long before you can take healthy DNA from a human donor and splice it into diseased organs?"

The scientist slid his glasses back on. The lenses acted as a shield to blur his eyes.

"Unfortunately we are years yet from human testing. Sulim, shall we show Ms. Chase and Dr. Wolfson BL-361? I think you'll find it most interesting, Mark."

Giving the fogged incubator a last, almost loving stroke, Hayes steered Mark toward the far end of the glass-fronted unit. Once again, his assistant activated some unseen mechanism and another incubator slid forward.

Taylor threw a last look at the pancreas and started to follow. What the hell...?

She thought at first that Dr. Hayes had left an imprint of his hand on the lid of the incubator.

The imprint was almost gone before Taylor's shocked mind accepted that the rapidly disappearing swirls were actually letters...and that they spelled out a desperate message.

### *Help!*

# Chapter 8

Dr. Hayes's message flashed like a neon sign inside Taylor's head throughout the rest of the lab tour.

The attentive Sulim Rasjan accompanied her, Mark and Dr. Hayes every step of the way. Hayes spoke mostly to Mark and avoided looking at Taylor directly.

After exiting the Regeneration Unit, they walked to the DNA Sequencing Facility. From there, they crossed to the Organic Synthesis Lab. They didn't go into the actual lab, but merely looked through a glass window at two white-coated techs working under an umbrellalike hood that vented the fumes from the chemicals they were mixing.

"This is where we produce the chemicals necessary for our research. As you can see, Diederik has spared no expense equipping the facilities."

The understatement of the year, Taylor thought as Hayes talked them through an array of equipment that included a preparative chromatography system, an infrared spectrometer and the racks of the glassware required for carrying out organic syntheses.

"Is this where you produce the preserving fluids used in the incubators?" she asked, her nose wrinkling despite the protective glass separating them from the unit's main floor.

"Yes, it is."

Hayes removed his glasses once more and polished them with a corner of his lab coat. A nervous habit, Taylor now suspected. Very nervous.

On pins and needles, she couldn't wait to get Mark somewhere she could tell him about the man's cry for help. She contained her impatience, though, until they exited the Organic Synthesis Lab.

"What's that?"

Her nod indicated a small building set some distance apart from the others inside the compound. Nestled in the shade of a towering banyan tree, it had no windows and a barred gate blocking its entrance.

"That is our clinic."

"Looks more like a prison," Taylor commented.

"Diederik retains a small medical staff," Oscar said without looking at her. "They see to the needs of the people here on the island."

The warning signals were shooting off like cluster bombs now. Before she could ask for a tour of the clinic, however, the cell phone clipped to Hayes's waistband beeped.

"That was Diederik," he explained after listening to a short message. "He and Beverly are waiting for us on the terrace. Sulim, please drive our guests back to the house. I'll follow shortly."

When Rasjan escorted Taylor and Mark to the golf cart, sheer desperation forced her to open the portal. Once seated, she turned her head to the side, closed her eyes and summoned the image of the rickety storage shed behind her grandparents' home. The gate had barely creaked open on its rusty hinges when she winged off an urgent signal.

*Mark! Dr. Hayes gave me a message!*

The golf cart hiccupped into motion. Taylor started to angle around to see if Mark had received her transmission when his reply slammed into her mind.

*When? How?*

*At the Regeneration Facility. He traced the word "help" in the mist on the incubator.*

*Help? Just that?*

*Just that.*

*Hell! I thought he seemed nervous, but I wrote it off to his admission that he and his crew are splicing animal DNA into human cells.*

*We need to get him alone, where he can talk or scribble notes. And there's something else. That medical clinic. I want to…*

"Hey, y'all!"

Bev's cheerful voice wrenched Taylor from the silent colloquy. Glancing up, she saw the blonde beckoning from the terrace.

"You're just in time for cocktails."

Their hostess had changed into filmy, flame-colored palazzo pants and a matching sequined tank that hugged her voluptuous breasts. The layers of chiffon in the wide-legged pants floated on the island breeze as she ran an approving eye over Taylor in her borrowed garb.

"Glad to see the slacks fit you." Her smile bright, she waved her guests to wrought-iron stools grouped around an L-shaped bar. "So, what'd y'all think of Diederik's lab?"

"Very impressive," Mark answered.

"Him 'n Oscar have tried to explain to me what they're doing in the compound," the blonde confessed, "but they might as well be talkin' Chinese." Holding up her frosted glass, she tinkled the half-melted ice. "I'll have another while you're fixin' one for Taylor and Mark, Diederik."

"Certainly, darling."

In contrast to his flamboyant wife, van Deursen looked almost colorless in his white slacks and panama shirt. Moving with languid grace, he reached across the bar for her glass.

The two certainly took the prize for one of the world's most contrasting couples, Taylor thought. Yet they seemed happy enough. Bev's eyes held nothing but puppy-dog adoration when they rested on her husband. He, in turn, had gifted his bride with a trousseau fit for a princess and was apparently working behind the scenes to polish off a few of her rough edges.

Still…

Taylor would rather have Mark Wolfson curled up beside her in bed any day. Or night. Like, for instance, the one fast coming on.

Their sleeping arrangements hadn't really concerned her until she'd spied the net-draped bed in the guest suite. Up to that point she'd been too busy with trifling matters like, oh, convincing Mark to accompany her to the Caribbean, smashing a sloop on a treacherous reef, and busting up a possible human organs black market ring.

Even after the king-size bed had snagged her attention, she'd shrugged it off with the reminder that she'd infiltrated van Deursen's island for a specific purpose—one that did *not* include getting all warm and cuddly with Mark Wolfson.

*If our room is in fact bugged, doesn't look like you'll have much choice.*

Too late she realized she'd forgotten to close the portal. Again! She glanced at Mark, caught the sardonic gleam in his eyes and kicked the damned gate shut.

The rattle of ice cubes drew her attention back to van Deursen. "What would you two like?" he asked as he tipped a pitcher and filled Bev's glass with a frosty mixture.

"That looks good," Taylor replied. "What is it?"

"Passion fruit daiquiris. This pitcher is nonalcoholic, but I've mixed another with Brinley Gold, a rum produced here in St. Kitts."

"Brinley is smoother than a baby's butt," Bev assured her. "The owner of the dump where I used to work would keep a bottle on the shelf behind the bar for show. Sleazy bastard would always refill it with the cheap stuff." She threw a look of longing at the bar cart. "Sure would like one little splash."

"Of course, darling. If you're certain that's what you want…"

Bev heaved a sigh. "I guess not. We're trying to get pregnant," she confided to Mark and Taylor. "Oscar suggested we cut out the booze, as it inhibits the hormone or enzyme or whatever it is that triggers sex."

Interesting, Taylor thought, since booze seemed to have the opposite effect on most people.

It had certainly triggered a few near-orgies in her younger, wilder college years.

Not that alcohol had played any part in her seduction of and by her zoology professor. She hadn't needed any artificial stimulant, she recalled, sliding Mark a sideways glance.

How long ago that fiasco seemed now. The anger and hurt she'd felt then dimmed a little more with each hour spent in Mark's company. Vaguely uncomfortable with the thought, she opted for a non-alcoholic daiquiri.

"Mark and I opened a bottle of the champagne you left in our suite and toasted our rescue. That's all the booze I can handle on a near empty stomach."

Particularly with Oscar Hayes's message still front and center in her mind. The single word had erased any doubt that van Deursen or his wife or both had engineered the scientist's sudden visit to the island and were holding him against his will in their tropical paradise.

Now all Taylor had to do was get him out of it.

With various extraction plans swirling around in her head, she accepted the frosted glass van Deursen handed to her. A chagrined Bev shoved a tray of fruit and cheese along the marble-topped bar.

"I didn't think 'bout y'all being hungry. Here, chow down on these goodies 'n I'll tell the chef to put a rush job on dinner."

"I'll do it," her husband said. "Just let me fix Mark a drink."

Van Deursen relayed the order via a house phone set in a convenient niche. He took the stool beside Beverly's, at a comfortable conversational angle to his guests. They might have been four friends gathered to share the onset of a balmy tropical evening, Taylor thought as she sipped her passion fruit icy. The drink was tart on her tongue and gloriously cold going down.

"Did Oscar walk you through the Regeneration Unit?" van Deursen asked.

"He did," Mark replied. "Also the DNA Sequencing Unit and the Organic Synthesis Lab. I'm curious, Diederik. Did you construct those extensive facilities here, on your own island, to avoid governmental oversight into the research your people are conducting?"

"In part," he admitted without a blush. "I'm sure you can understand why. From what Oscar told me of your own research, I venture to say you, too, have been severely constrained by controls imposed by Washington bureaucrats."

"Of course."

He flicked a glance in Taylor's direction. She sipped her drink and pretended total amnesia in regard to her threat to put a hold on his government grants.

"But without those controls and oversight, you'll face an uphill battle getting the results of your research into the U.S. market."

"There are other markets," van Deursen said, unperturbed by the prospect. "Africa, for example, and India. The great masses of poor on those continents would benefit from drugs synthesized with more speed and less cost."

"Not if they ultimately proved unsafe."

"True. Which is why I asked Oscar to assume direction of the facilities here. His reputation is as unassailable as his standards are rigorous." His glance measured Mark thoughtfully, carefully. "Oscar says you have a brilliant mind, Dr. Wolfson, and an intellectual curiosity that's led you into new, rather daring fields of research. I admire that kind of enterprising spirit. I've also done some quick investigations into your work. I'm very interested in how the power of the mind might influence the body's ability to heal itself. Perhaps you might consider joining my team? Taylor as well, of course."

Bev cooed with delight at the prospect, but Mark merely hooked a brow. "We're working on some critical programs at Princeton."

"I'm sure you are. Just think about it and we'll talk more tomorrow. Ah, here's George. Hopefully to announce our dinner."

The white-jacketed cook's helper had indeed come with word that appetizers and salad could be served whenever they wished.

"We're ready now. Beverly, my dearest, why don't you lead the way?"

Hooking her arm through Mark's, Bev bounced up the short flight of flagstone steps with complete disregard for her strappy, three-inch sandals. Taylor's flat-heeled boat shoes made the ascent easier. Even so, van Deursen took it slowly and had to pause two steps from the top.

"Are you all right?" she asked, eyeing the sudden sheen of sweat on his upper lip.

"I am. Truly." He summoned an apologetic

smile and ascended the last two stairs. "Just not quite as young as I used to be."

Taylor matched her pace to his as they followed Bev and Mark to the dining room. Its floor-to-ceiling sliding glass panels stood open, and the spectacular chandelier beckoned with a hundred or more softly glowing lights. The silver candelabra bracketing both ends of a mahogany sideboard added their own flickering light to the exotic setting.

"Please," van Deursen murmured, patting his upper lip with a snowy linen handkerchief, "don't say anything to Beverly. She tends to fuss."

Taylor didn't have to say anything. Her hostess took one look at her husband's face and immediately jumped out of the chair Mark had pulled out for her.

"Diederik! Baby! Do you need a shot?"

"I'm fine."

"No, you ain't." Worry thickened her accent and erased any concern for grammar or syntax. "'Scuse us, folks. Y'all go ahead and eat." Grabbing her husband's arm, she practically dragged him from the dining room. "Diederik 'n me will just step out for a little while."

Taylor knew any unseen watchers or listeners would expect her to comment on the obvious. Accordingly she broke the small silence that followed the couple's abrupt withdrawal.

"Well, I guess we know now why Diederik van Deursen spent millions to set up his own private research facilities."

Not to sell engineered organs on the black market, she now suspected, although that might be an offshoot, but to provide himself with an immediately available bank of body parts should he need them.

"What do you think he has?"

"I've no idea," Mark answered slowly.

They stood for several moments, each lost in thought, until the white-jacketed servant who'd summoned them to dinner arrived with a silver tray. He didn't appear overly surprised to find they'd been deserted by their host and hostess. Word traveled with the speed of light—or video surveillance—in the van Deursen household.

"Is Dr. Hayes joining us?" Mark asked, eyeing the fifth place setting.

"No, sir. He rang the house to say he's been detained at the lab."

So it was just Taylor and Mark at the long table. If Oscar Hayes's desperate message wasn't front and center in her consciousness, she might have been seduced by the incredible setting.

Outside the open windows, the sea turned from turquoise to cobalt, with iridescent waves curling into the shore. Candlelight wove patterns on the dining room wall each time the breeze whispered in. A Vivaldi concerto provided an elegant counterpoint to the pool water that spilled from one tier to another in a seductive patter.

And the meal. Dear God, the meal.

As she worked her way from a clear consommé through a fresh spinach salad and perfectly broiled red snapper to a crème brûlée that made her taste buds want to weep with joy, Taylor decided that whatever Diederik van Deursen paid his chef, it wasn't enough. The attentive server offered wine with each course, but both she and Mark stuck with iced tea during dinner and coffee afterward.

Beverly reappeared while Taylor was licking the last of the luscious custard and caramelized sugar from her spoon. Clearly shaken, the blonde dropped into her chair.

"Sorry I ducked out on you, folks. Diederik

has these…these little spells every once in a while."

"Is he all right?"

"Yeah." She pushed back her champagne colored bangs. "The doc gave him a shot. He's sleepin' like a baby."

"What causes his spells, Bev?"

She hesitated, gnawing on her lower lip. Taylor suspected van Deursen had made his wife sign a confidentiality statement, just as he had his employees.

"He… He probably wouldn't want me to say nuthin'. He's downright paranoid about his personal life. But he don't—*doesn't*—want me to worry and Oscar just confuses me with all his technical terms." Her brown eyes pleaded with Mark. "Maybe you can put it in words I can understand."

"I'll try."

"He's got a blood disease. His momma had the same sickness." She plucked the napkin from her empty plate and rolled it into a rope, twisting and untwisting it nervously. "It's called hemo-chromo…hemo-chrota…"

"Hemochromatosis?" Mark prompted.

"That's the little bugger! You know about it?"

"I know it's an inherited disorder that causes the body to absorb more iron than it needs. With no natural way to rid itself of the excess iron, the body stores it in various organs, most notably the liver, pancreas and heart. In advanced stages, the disease affects the brain, the lungs and every other organ."

Images of van Deursen's high-tech incubators filled Taylor's mind. Surely he couldn't be growing a spare brain and an extra set of lungs, too?

"The usual treatment for hemochromatosis is a phlebotomy," Mark continued, "drawing a pint of blood every few weeks to lower the fermin levels."

"He's been doin' that! The doc sucks it out of him like a vampire. So why ain't he gettin' better?"

"Could be the disease had progressed too far before his doctors discovered it. Or he may have presented with other symptoms that masked it. You'd better prepare yourself, Bev. If there's too much damage, he may be looking at multiple organ transplants."

"That's... That's what I thought." The linen

napkin twisted in her white-knuckled hands. "'Cept…his chances of gettin' a match for a heart 'n a liver 'n a pancreas and new lungs can't be real good. He's O negative, like me, but his blood type's got this whole string of initials after it. Oscar says there ain't…*aren't*…more 'n a handful of people in the whole world with that type."

She gnawed on her lower lip, chewing off all trace of lipstick.

"You saw what Oscar's doing in the Regeneration Unit," she said hesitantly. "Both of you. Do you think…? Would you risk…?" Gulping, she appealed to Mark. "I mean, if it was Taylor and she had no other options, would you skirt around government restrictions?"

The questions hung over the table like a noxious cloud. Bev might not know the specifics of the laws that governed human test protocols but she had to realize her husband didn't intend to just skirt around them. From the sound of it, he would disregard them completely if necessary.

So, it turned out, would Mark. Leaning forward, he cut through the ethical issues with the clean, swift slice of a scalpel.

"If it was Taylor, I'd do anything in my power

to help her, legal or otherwise. But I'd make very, very sure I didn't destroy her in the process."

Taylor mulled over his reply until Bev apologized and pushed back her chair. Offering them the use of the theater room or spa, she retired to look after Diederik. Her guests lingered in the dining room until the efficient attendant produced a heaping bowl of hamburger meat for Tikal, which they carried back to the guest suite.

While the dog gobbled down his dinner, Taylor kicked off her shoes, rolled up her pant legs, and plopped down on the ledge of the pool that lapped into the guest suite. Lit from below, the water swirled golden green around her calves.

Mark joined her. Hip to hip, shoulder to shoulder, they used the cover of Tikal's noisy slurping to confirm that their first order of business was to let Oscar know they'd come specifically for him. Their second, to get him the hell off the island.

Tikal finished his dinner before they could discuss how best to accomplish both objectives. Licking his chops, the dog came over and butted Mark's arm.

"You need a run to loosen the kinks, don't you, fella? Me, too, but I think we'll have to settle for a short walk tonight. Be back shortly, Taylor."

She swished her leg in the pool, watching man and dog make their way to the lower level of the terrace. Tikal sniffed the unfamiliar scents, went into the undergrowth, and rattled the bushes. His exploration must have tripped a silent alarm, as spotlights blinked on and the entire garden lit up like a runway. Mere seconds later, two men in black T-shirts and jungle fatigue pants converged on the scene.

Tikal went immediately into attack mode. Ears back, fangs bared, he dropped into a crouch. Taylor saw one of the guards whip up the weapon slung over his shoulder and started to shout a warning, but Mark had already intervened.

"It's okay! He's with me."

Slowly the watchman lowered his weapon. Tikal remained in a crouch as Mark attempted to make peace.

"Sorry about tripping the lights. I should have asked Bev or Diederik where to walk him. We'll head back into the house now. Tikal, let's go."

The dog rose but before following Mark, he

padded to a palm tree a few feet from the nearest guard and lifted his leg. The spray arced, glistening in the bright floodlights, and splashed when it hit the scaly trunk. Cursing, the guard leaped to the side.

Taylor bit her lip. Under any other circumstances she would have been grinning from ear to ear. But when the guard jumped, she got a good look at his weapon.

The men who'd come out to rescue them from the raft had carried sidearms and an assortment of police-type paraphernalia. This guy was toting a Heckler & Koch military-style assault weapon, one of the new, lightweight Commando versions that could be fitted with an under-barrel grenade launcher.

The prospect of getting Dr. Hayes off van Deursen's island without calling for a full-scale invasion by a joint U.S.-St. Kitts task force suddenly seemed a whole lot more remote.

Mark's expression when he strode into the guest suite told Taylor he'd gotten an eyeful, too. His jaw tight, he closed and locked the sliding glass doors.

"It's been one helluva day. I'm too tired to wait for Oscar. Let's go to bed."

# Chapter 9

The image of that lethal, military-style assault weapon stayed with Taylor as she retreated to the bathroom and let her borrowed negligee slither over her breasts and hips.

She itched to dig out her cell phone and provide Sergeant Powell and Constable Benjamin with a situational assessment but couldn't risk it until she got away from the house.

She also *had* to catch Oscar Hayes when he returned to his suite in the guest wing. If she missed the sound of his footsteps in the hall, Tikal would surely catch them. When the dog alerted them, she and Mark would get up, throw on a robe and invite the doc to their suite for a drink. Van Deursen's extraordinary request for Mark to join his team provided the perfect excuse for a late-night chat. During the discussion, Taylor would resort to scribbled notes or hand signals to communicate her real identity to Oscar.

In the meantime, she'd snatch a few hours' rest. As Mark said, it had been a helluva day. They could both use a short breather to regroup and recharge.

That was the plan, anyway—until she emerged from the bathroom and caught sight of Mark. He was already in bed, his back against the massive wooden headboard, his hands locked behind his neck. The cotton sheet covered him to the waist. Above it, his bare chest showed a light dusting of black hair that arrowed down to…

Whoa! Stop right there, girl!

Taylor slapped a chokehold on her thoughts. She had no business tracking the man's chest hair. And she sure didn't need to go all dopey over a patch of bronzed skin and some sinewy muscles. She'd gotten an eyeful of both in the past twenty-four hours. Still, she had to force air into her lungs as she flicked off the bathroom light.

Mark watched her approach, his blue eyes skimming the lace-trimmed black negligee. "Nice."

"It's part of Bev's trousseau."

Suddenly, ridiculously self-conscious, she resisted the urge to tug up the low-cut bodice. Thankfully the lace contained a hint of spandex that kept it from sagging like a feed sack on her.

With a nod to Tikal, stretched out by the sliding glass doors, she slid into the king-size bed and tugged up the sheet. If they *were* being monitored, she and Mark would have to cuddle, but she was damned if she'd give any of van Deursen's goons another free show.

She snapped off the lamp on her side of the bed. Mark did the same on his. The bedroom sank into a gloom lit only by the thin slice of moon showing in the fanlight above the closed plantation shutters.

This was an operational necessity, she told herself as she inched across the half acre of cloud-soft sheet. A military requirement. All part of her mission.

Yeah, sure! Like anyone would believe that,

Taylor included. All she had to do was nestle her head on Mark's shoulder to admit this rush of heat owed nothing to military necessity.

He curled her closer, his fingers playing with the ends of her hair, but made no other move. Taylor should have been relieved. Instead the insidious heat kicked up another few degrees. It was the feel of his skin smooth and warm against her cheek, she decided. The slow rise and fall of his chest beneath her cheek.

Driven by an impulse she knew was insane, she splayed a hand against that broad expanse. The crinkly hair tickled her palm. The urge to slide her hand lower bit at her, but Taylor managed to beat this one into submission. She couldn't stop herself from asking the question that had dogged her since dinner, though.

"Did you mean what you said? About doing anything for me?"

The fingers playing with the ends of her hair stilled. "Yes."

She angled her head, trying to read his expression. The gloom masked it. "Legal or otherwise?"

"Yes."

She wanted to ask if that included getting into

the head of a teasing coed and beating her at her own, seductive game. But she was reluctant to destroy this island of calm in their otherwise turbulent day.

She should have known Mark wouldn't let it go at that. Cradling her head in his hand, he leaned over her. His breath was warm on her cheeks, his shoulders a solid wall in the darkness.

"What about you, Taylor? Did you mean that back in Princeton, when you said you'd fallen for an uptight zoology professor who played you like one of Pavlov's dogs?"

She hadn't *said* it, she recalled. Not verbally. But she didn't want to correct him and advertise to any possible listeners that Mark could troop around inside her head.

"That was a long time ago," she muttered. "And 'falling for' is a very loose term."

"So define it. Give me the precise parameters, and put them in a current perspective."

She stared up into his shadowed face. "Are you asking whether I'd do anything for you?"

Her first instinct was to brush the question aside. Reluctantly she quashed it. She owed him—

and herself—an honest answer. Assuming she could reach deep enough inside herself to find one.

She wanted him. She couldn't lie to herself about that, or to Mark. She ached to lock her arms around his neck and draw his head down to hers. The need rose with every wash of his breath against her mouth, every thud of the heart beating against her palm.

Yet this tangle of emotion he roused in her involved more than just animal attraction, more than mere hunger. These past days had rekindled the respect and admiration she'd once held for him, along with a sneaking suspicion she could tumble into love with the man again if she let herself.

Maybe she already had. Just a little. But this wasn't the time or the place to take whatever she was feeling to the next level. Lifting her hand, she laid it against his cheek.

"Ask me again," she whispered, "when we get home."

When they didn't have to worry someone might be recording every word. When she'd had time to sort through the conflicting emotions he stirred and the press of his lean, hard body wasn't tripping every one of her circuit breakers.

"I'll hold you to that."

Brushing his mouth over hers, he shifted her in his arms until they were stretched out on the bed, her back to his front. He held her loosely, his thighs tucked into hers.

It should have ended there. Taylor was sure it had. She lay wide-eyed in the darkness, listening to the murmur of the sea outside, willing away the tension that had her knotted up like macramé. She rolled her shoulders, trying to loosen the kinks, and realized Mark was as tense as she was.

She could feel him where their bodies connected. His muscles remained stiff and rock-hard. All of them, she noted with a sudden constriction in her throat, including the one that poked at her backside.

She squirmed, her breath hissing out.

Mark's hissed in.

He shifted behind her. Intentionally or otherwise, his knee slid between Taylor's and hitched upward. The pressure at the juncture of her thighs sent a jolt through her, hot and erotic and intense.

She must have gasped, a low throaty sound she hoped to God didn't carry beyond the bed.

It carried to Mark, though. He went absolutely still. The seconds ticked by. Three. Four. Until Taylor yielded to sheer insanity and squeezed his thigh between hers.

He didn't make a sound. Merely drew her closer and used his free hand to tug the sheet up to cover her shoulders. If her nightgown came up with the sheet, no one could tell except Taylor.

She lay as stiff as a board, hardly daring to breathe as his hand curved over her bare hip. She could tell when he discovered she was wearing a thong. He covered his small, almost inaudible grunt of surprise and delight by burying his face in her hair.

*Let me in, Taylor.*

Was she hearing him, or the echo of her own need? Unsure, she opened the gate. His voice came to her in the dark stillness.

*Are you protected?*

She knew she had to stop it then, or not at all. All she had to do was lie, tell him she wasn't on the Pill.

*Yes.*

*Let me in,* he said again, soft and seductive.

With a sigh, she rolled over and surrendered to his touch. Her head went back, exposing her throat to his teeth and tongue while his thumb teased her nipple. When he'd worked it into a tight bud, he moved to her other breast.

This was crazy. Sheer idiocy! She knew the room was bugged either for sound or video. Yet they were completely covered by the sheet and Mark didn't make a sound as he kneaded her aching flesh.

Taylor breathed through her mouth to keep from panting aloud as his hand slid down again, over her belly, under the waistband. He tugged the thong down, slowly, silently, using first his hands, then his knee. The sheets didn't so much as rustle as Taylor worked one leg free of the panties, but by then her blood was pounding so fast and loud she wouldn't have heard an F-16 kick into afterburner. Swallowing a groan, she canted her hips and eased her thighs apart.

He came into her with slow deliberation. She could feel every ridge and pulsing vein, feel him stretching her, filling her, and had to fight to keep from grinding her hips into his.

With his arm clamped around her waist, he anchored her against him while he eased out, then in, then out again. His movements were so quiet that not even Tikal stirred, and so damned erotic that Taylor had to bite down hard on her lower lip as sensation piled on top of sensation.

He must have sensed how close she was to the edge. With a smooth, silent play of muscle and strength, he thrust in, then tightened his arm and held her immobile. She felt her own muscles clench around him as the heat in her belly begin to spread.

She fought the climax, wanting to spin out the pleasure, but she couldn't control it. Still locked against him, she rode the dark, exquisite waves.

Mark almost lost it then. With Taylor's body locked against his, her ragged breath a mere whisper in the darkness, he wanted to shove upward, over and over, until she screamed his name.

Instead he gritted his teeth and held himself rigid until she shuddered and went limp. Only then did he move. A single, silent thrust that drained everything he had.

The sound of heavy breathing dragged Taylor from total unconsciousness.

Mark. It had to be Mark. She could still feel his arm heavy across her waist, his body warm at her back.

She lay with her eyes closed while her mind slowly reengaged. She couldn't quite believe she'd just experienced the most explosive orgasm of her life. The fact that she'd remained silent during total meltdown inside no doubt contributed to the intensity of her...

"Uh!"

She gasped, prodded into full wakefulness by the application of something cold and hard against her left breast. Her startled gaze locked with a pair of ice-blue eyes.

"Dammit, Tikal!"

"What?" Shaken awake, Mark tightened his arm reflexively. "What?"

"Your dog," Taylor muttered. "One of these days he's going to stick his nose in the wrong place and get it seriously rearranged."

Only when Tikal dropped onto his haunches, tongue lolling in a grin, did she remember that she'd been counting on the animal to growl or bark and let them know when Oscar Hayes returned to his suite.

Judging by the hazy light streaming through the

shutters, her early warning system had failed. She and Mark hadn't just dozed off, they'd slept through the night.

"Some watchdog you are."

Glaring at the animal, Taylor tossed aside the sheet. Her borrowed nightgown had twisted around her hips and required some untangling as she slid out of bed.

"Maybe we can catch Oscar before we join the van Deursen's for breakfast," she said with deliberate nonchalance. "I know you want to tell him about Diederik's suggestion you join the team."

Belted into the robes provided by their thoughtful hosts, she and Mark crossed through the guest wing's kitchen, living room and entertainment areas. The doors to two other bedroom suites stood open, displaying their lack of occupancy. When they knocked on the third, they received no answer.

Disappointed and frustrated, Taylor accompanied Mark back to their suite. While he took Tikal out on the terrace, she scrubbed down and dressed in her own shorts and red tank top. The clothes were freshly laundered by van Deursen's efficient staff and waiting on the console table outside the suite. The reef had shredded Mark's shirt beyond repair, however, so he made do with another colorful tropical shirt and borrowed huaraches.

When they made their way along the breezeway that led to the main part of the house, the sun wasn't as brilliant as it had been yesterday but the humidity was a killer. Angry gray clouds had piled up out to sea. Dumping sheets of rain, the distant shower looked as though it might hang around for a while.

"Hey, y'all!"

Beverly was seated at the glass-topped table on the upper tier of the terrace. Her greeting was as bright as her tiger lily-print caftan, but tired lines were etched at the corners of her eyes.

"How's Diederik?" Taylor asked as she and Mark joined their hostess.

"Better this morning. It was kinda rough for a while last night, though, so I'm just lettin' him sleep a while. Y'all want coffee or tea?"

"Coffee for me," Taylor replied.

"Me, as well."

She lifted a hand to signal the uniformed servant lingering unobtrusively off to one side of the terrace and dropped it again, wincing.

"Are *you* okay, Bev?"

"I just got a little twitch in my back. George, fresh coffee for Mz. Chase and Dr. Wolfson, please."

"Yes, madam."

He filled two cups from a silver pot, offered cream and sugar and set a basket of freshly baked croissants next to a platter of tropical fruit.

"What would you like for breakfast?" Bev inquired. "The chef kin do anything you want, but I gotta tell you his eggs Florentine are really something special." Her mouth curved. "I thought I'd gag first time I seen all that spinach and goopy egg yolk mixed together. Diederik made me try it, though, 'n now I'm hooked."

Despite the somewhat less than appetizing description, both guests went with the chef's special.

"Did y'all sleep okay?"

Taylor almost choked on her first sip of the fragrant Costa Rican blend. She could hardly admit she'd dropped into total unconsciousness after one of the most intensely erotic experiences of her life.

She'd have to sort out the implications of that incredible coupling later. Right now she settled for burying her nose in her coffee cup as Mark answered for both of them.

"Very well, thanks. Will Oscar be joining us for breakfast? I'd like to consult with him a little more about his work."

"I'm not sure." Bev edged from side to side in her chair, as if trying to remove the kink in her back. "He, uh, was at the lab pretty late last night."

"Taylor and I knocked on his door before we came down for breakfast but got no answer. Has he already gone back to the lab?"

"Probably." She didn't quite meet Mark's eyes. "Oscar's real dedicated to his work."

She knew!

Taylor cradled her raised coffee cup in both hands to hide her sudden, absolute conviction. There wasn't a doubt in her mind now. Beverly van Deursen *knew* Hayes was on the island under duress. No wonder she'd stammered out that sad, brokenhearted spiel last night about taking risks and having no other options.

Taylor felt sorry for her. Almost.

The woman had endured some hard breaks before her prince swooped in and carried her off to a life of unparalleled luxury. Now that life was falling apart before her eyes. Of course she'd conspire with the husband she seemed to love so much to save him any way she could.

The utter selfishness of her love was what killed Taylor's sympathy. Van Deursen wasn't the only seriously ill person in the world. Others suffered and endured unimaginable pain, her brother among them. Oscar Hayes's research could benefit more than just a single, ruthless billionaire.

And it damned well would, she vowed fiercely. More determined than ever to get the scientist off this island, Taylor contained her impatience through croissants, fruit, fresh squeezed juice, sugar-cured ham steaks and the admittedly spectacular eggs Florentine.

Her first order of business, she decided when they'd finished, was to contact Sergeant Powell and provide him a situational update. For that she needed to get away from the surveillance cameras sweeping the house and grounds. Tikal offered the perfect excuse.

"We usually take the dog for a run in the morning," she told Bev. "I couldn't jog after this gargantuan breakfast if my life depended on it, but we might go down to the beach and let him chase waves if you don't mind."

"Of course not. But you don't have to go 'way down to the cove. There's a jogging trail laid out behind the tennis courts."

All no doubt swept by cameras and silent alarms.

"Tikal isn't much for sticking to the beaten path," Mark said calmly, guessing Taylor's intent. "Which you probably realized last night when he went into the bushes and tripped an alarm. The whole terrace lit up. I hope it didn't wake you or Diederik."

Once again, Bev wouldn't quite meet his eyes. "We weren't asleep."

She made a terrible liar. Guilt and something else, something Taylor couldn't quite interpret, flickered across her face.

"Y'all have a good walk. I'll go check on Diederik. Hopefully he'll be up 'n about when you get back."

When she swirled her chair around and rose, a shadow of pain crossed her face. Then the cowl neck of her colorful caftan dipped in back, and Taylor spotted the reason for her grimace.

"Good God, Bev!"

Startled, her hostess glanced around. "What?"

"How did you get that bruise?"

The blonde clapped a hand to the back of her neck. Dismay flooded her chocolate-brown eyes. "I… I, uh, banged into a cupboard door."

Like hell she had!

"Let me see it. You might need to put some ice on the swelling."

Hastily Bev yanked up the caftan's cowl collar. "It's nothing. Just a bump. I gotta go check on Diederik. Y'all have a good walk."

# Chapter 10

Taylor and Mark said little as they descended the zigzagging stairs that led to the marina. At the bottom of the stairs they took the vine-shaded path that curved around to the van Deursens' private beach. Tikal roamed ahead, leaving his mark so many times Taylor might have marveled at his seemingly endless ability to lift his leg if Bev's injury hadn't occupied her thoughts.

She'd caught only a glimpse of the ugly bruise, but she'd dealt with enough drug addicts in her career as an undercover agent to recognize the edema that often accompanied an intramuscular injection. The puncture mark was another sure clue.

Except Bev would have to be a contortionist to reach around and shoot up at the base of her neck like that. Obviously someone else had given her the shot. Taylor was sure the injection was related in some way to Diederik's illness, but how? And what the hell kind of needle would make such a vicious bruise?

Itching for answers, she plopped down onto the sand and unlaced her shoes while Mark shed his shirt and sandals. Selecting a suitable piece of deadwood, he launched the stick into the surf. Tikal barked joyously and plunged in to retrieve it.

With man and dog engaged in what looked like a familiar routine, Taylor peeled back the insole of her left shoe and hit star six. Sergeant Powell had obviously been waiting for the contact. He answered within seconds.

"Go ahead, Captain."

She doubted anyone could hear her over the noise of the surf and the dog, but she let the shoe drop to the sand and looped her wrists over her upraised knees. Looking like a woman with nothing better to do than watch her man splash through the waves, she barely moved her lips.

"The situation is pretty much as we suspected. Hayes is here under duress."

"How and when do you want to get him out?"

"I haven't decided on the when yet. As to the how, van Deursen's private navy maintains several high-powered boats. I'm thinking it might be less risky to appropriate one of those than call in a chopper and extraction team. His guys pack some real firepower."

If the submachine gun she'd spotted last night was any indication of their arsenal, van Deursen's goons could put up a hell of a fight.

"We have authority to pull in additional assets if necessary," Powell reminded her. "The *U.S.S. Enterprise* is on patrol out of Gitmo. Her Seahawks can provide all the fire suppression you need."

The Seahawk was the navy version of the army's Blackhawk and the air force's Pave Hawk helicopters. Armed with machine guns, Hellfire missiles, torpedoes and a .50 caliber cannon, the 'Hawk could blast away half of van Deursen's island.

In addition to American assets, Nigel Benjamin had pledged aid from St. Kitts's constabulary and home guard if Taylor verified Hayes was being held against his will. All she had to do was say the word.

She weighed the options and came down on the side of caution. "I think I can accomplish our objective without a full-scale assault."

"Your call, Captain, but you might have to factor something else into your exit strategy. There's a tropical depression forming in the south Atlantic."

"Oh, great!"

"They're saying it could blow into a real bitch of a storm."

Her gaze whipped to the clouds dumping rain far out to sea. Did they represent just a localized shower or a precursor of worse to come?

"Is it headed this way?"

"Too early to tell, but she's gathering sound and fury as we speak."

"She?"

"Next name on the hurricane list is Gail."

Just what she needed. Hurricane Gail wreaking havoc and destruction.

Swiftly Taylor assessed the possible ramifications. Van Deursen's people would be tracking the weather. They'd have an evacuation plan all worked out. Taylor would have to scope out their plan and decide how she could use it to her advantage. In the meantime, she needed Powell to do a little digging.

"We found out last night van Deursen is suffering from an illness called he-mo-chro-ma-to-sis." She said the term slowly, giving him time to jot it down. "See if you can find out where and when he's been treated for it and what the prognosis is. Run a med-check on his wife, too."

"Will do."

"I'll get back to you when I can."

"Roger."

Appearing to play idly with the shoe, she ended the transmission and nudged the insole into place. She was still turning over the implications of a possible hurricane in her mind when Mark called a halt to the surf splashing. With salt spray glistening in his black hair and his wet shorts molding his hips, he waded back up on the beach.

Tikal panted up with him and planted all four paws before sending his body into a series of massive shakes that spewed sand and seawater in all directions. Unperturbed by the onslaught, Mark stretched out beside Taylor.

She swiped Tikal spray from her face and leaned down on one elbow. To any observer they would look like two lovers lazing on a beach. She added to the picture by using her fingers to nudge back the hair that had fallen across Mark's forehead.

"We may have a problem," she murmured.

"What's that?"

"Powell says there's a storm building in the south Atlantic. It could blow into a hurricane."

"Wonderful."

"That's pretty much what I said, too."

"So what's the plan? Do we ride out the storm with the van Deursens or move up the timetable?"

"I'm thinking we'd better move up the time-table. We have to get to Hayes today and let him know what's happening."

Lightly she dusted away the sand sprinkled across his shoulders and chest. The small corner of her mind not totally absorbed by the urgency of their mission noted the damp heat of his skin.

"I also want into the marina," she told him.

"We can use the excuse of checking to see if van Deursen's men have salvaged anything from the sloop to get our feet in the door."

"Why do you want in?"

"We may have to appropriate one of their boats instead of calling in an extraction team. I'm not sure I want to risk getting the team caught in a crossfire."

His jaw tightening, Mark stared up into her green eyes. He didn't pretend to know anything about submachine guns, but the one the guard was toting last night had made a decided impression.

"I don't particularly care for the idea of a cross-fire, either."

Or for his gut certainty that Taylor would be right in the middle of it, directing the operation.

He still hadn't assessed his feelings about what had happened between them last night. Part of him hated that they'd had to restrain their re-sponses and keep the damned sheet drawn up to their necks. He'd ached to roll her over, spread-eagle her on the bed and expose every inch of her body to his hands and mouth. Yet even with their self-imposed restraints, she'd destroyed any last, lingering thought that he could let her walk away from him again. He wanted this woman any way he could have her. But preferably alive.

His overriding instinct was to hustle her off this island and back to nice, safe, secure Princeton. Not that she'd stay there, Mark acknowledged grimly. If—*when*—they worked out a future that included *un*restrained nights, he knew he'd have to subdue his primal urge to shield and protect his mate. He'd also have to live with the knowledge that Taylor's chosen profession put her in harm's way.

Like now, when she was calmly proposing they hijack one of van Deursen's high-powered speed-boats and depart the island, very likely under a hail of gunfire. The prospect put a kink in Mark's gut he suspected continued association with Taylor would soon make permanent.

"We'll check out the boathouse on our way back, then track down Oscar." Shoving his hands through her hair, he dragged her head down. "Just promise me you won't take any unnecessary risks."

"I wouldn't last long in this job if I did."

"Promise me," he ordered in a tone so fierce Tikal's head popped up. The sight of the two humans locked together brought the dog to his feet. With a questioning nudge, he pushed between them.

"Sorry, pal." Lifting a shoulder, Mark shoved him out of the circle. "This is between the two of us."

Taylor's instinct was to resist the pressure he was exerting. She'd been her own woman for so long, it went against the grain to yield to a man— especially a man who'd betrayed her trust once.

Yet she'd yielded to Mark last night, physically and emotionally. For those brief moments, she'd shut her mind to everything else and let herself go. Not real smart for someone charged with a potentially dangerous mission. Which brought her back to Mark's demand.

"I promise I won't take any unnecessary risks."

As she'd already stated, she wouldn't last long in her profession if she did. She suspected, however, that her definition of unnecessary and Mark's might differ considerably depending on the circumstances.

He took her at her word, however, and leaned in. "Just to seal the bargain…"

The kiss was hard and fast, a hint of things to

come when they didn't have to measure each word or watch every move. Taylor held nothing back as she returned it.

One of van Deursen's men stopped Taylor and Mark at the entrance to the marina.

"Mr. van Deursen offered us the use of a boat," Mark told him.

"Yes, sir. Just let me verify that with my boss."

Once cleared, Mark signaled Tikal to stay while the guard showed him and Taylor through the extremely well-equipped marina. It contained everything necessary for the aquatic entertainment of van Deursen and his guests, from a small fleet of jet-skis, windsurfers and speedboats to a forty-foot Infinity Sport bristling with rods and reels for deep sea fishing. Docked next to the Infinity was a high-speed launch similar to the one that had sped to their rescue after the *Ocean Breeze* hit the reef. At the far end of the dock was the helipad, with a sleek JetRanger III securely tied down.

Taylor divided her interest between the boats, the helicopter and the array of surveillance cameras, infrared sensors and motion detectors protecting them. She also took special note of the gas pump located middock.

"The *Oriana* is in here," their escort said as he punched in a code beside the entrance to the boathouse.

Van Deursen's gleaming white yacht ate up most of the space inside the cavernous facility. Suspended on hoists for dry storage and maintenance, the monster craft looked big enough to host the next Big Eight summit.

"Here is our operations center."

Punching in another access code, the guard showed them into the marina's nerve center. Glass windows gave sweeping views of the sea and the boat slips while monitors blipped with updates on weather and navigational notices. A large, dark-complexioned individual in camouflage pants and a black T-shirt swung his chair around and rose.

"Ms. Chase, Dr. Wolfson." He introduced himself with the musical lilt of the islands. "I'm Alex Yardley."

His hand was as big as the rest of him and leather tough. Taylor was sure she could take him down if she had to, but kind of hoped she wouldn't.

"Have you recovered from the ordeal of losing your boat?" Yardley asked.

"We have," Mark confirmed and followed

Taylor's suggested lead. "We thought we'd check and see if any of the property or equipment that was aboard her may have washed ashore or been salvaged by your men."

"Unfortunately all we've found are float cushions and pieces of wreckage."

"Then perhaps we could borrow a boat and some scuba tanks. We might be able to retrieve some of our gear."

"Are you dive certified?"

"We are."

His glance slid to Taylor, back to Mark. She guessed he was wondering why two people who were scuba qualified didn't have enough smarts to keep their boat clear of a reef marked on all navigational charts.

"Very well. Do you wish to go now?"

"I need to borrow a bathing suit first," Taylor answered, skimming a hand over her freshly laundered shorts and tank top. "Give us a half hour."

"Better not plan on staying out too long," he advised. "We're getting reports of a storm brewing to the southeast. It could be a bad one."

"What happens if it heads our way?"

"We have contingency plans in place."

Taylor wanted more than that bland assurance. "Do we fly out of the path of the storm or take the boats? Not that I'm worried, you understand. I'm just not real thrilled with the idea we might get caught in a typhoon and sink. Again."

"If it looks like the island might take a hit, we'll fly you out."

"To where?"

"Mr. van Deursen maintains a designated safe haven for just such a contingency."

She didn't like the way he dodged the question. She liked even less the idea of being transported to another secure lockdown and developing a new extraction plan.

They'd have to go today, she decided. This morning, if possible. With a last look around, she finalized her escape plan.

Neither Beverly nor her husband were in view when Taylor and Mark trudged up from the marina and went directly to the guest wing. The aroma of cherry blend tobacco was stronger this time, fresher. Taylor's pulse leaped. Hayes had come out for a smoke within the last few minutes. Maybe they'd finally catch him in his suite.

When he answered their knock on his door, Taylor sucked in a shocked breath. The scientist had appeared weary and decidedly nervous yesterday. This morning, his shoulders slumped and an unhealthy pallor made the liver spots dotting his face stand out in stark contrast. Even his frizzy gray hair drooped around his ears.

"Good Lord, Oscar." Mark made no attempt to hide his concern. "Are you okay?"

"I'm fine. Just a little tired."

"You don't look fine. You look almost as bad as van Deursen did yesterday evening. Beverly said at breakfast that he had a rough time. Did you stay with him all night?"

Tugging off his black-framed glasses, Hayes polished the bottle-thick lenses with a corner of his lab coat.

"Most of it."

"I can see this is a bad time, but we wanted to talk to you."

He looked up quickly. Fear paralyzed his features and drained what little blood was left in his face.

He assumed they'd come to discuss his cryptic message, Taylor realized. Flashing him a look that said she understood his fear, she rushed in with their cover story.

"Diederik invited Mark and me to join his team. We thought we'd get your take on it."

"Ah. Yes, of course." His Adam's apple bobbed with obvious relief. "He told me he'd extended the offer. Please come in and we'll discuss it."

His suite was as luxurious as the one Taylor and Mark occupied, but furnished with a more tropical flair. Where their furniture was heavy British colonial in dark mahogany, his incorporated lots of rattan and bright, breezy island prints. Hayes's pipe, tobacco pouch and plastic lighter lay at the ready on a round table with a twisted column pedestal.

As in Taylor and Mark's suite, the sliding glass panels gave a spectacular view of the sea. Taylor noted with interest that it also gave a different sweep of the grounds. While Hayes insisted on getting them something cold to drink and fussed at the minibar, she studied the low-roofed structures half hidden amid the jungle greenery.

"What are those?" she asked when the scientist thrust a glass of water and ice into her hand.

"Servants' quarters."

She counted at least twelve bungalows. There were probably a dozen more screened by the eucalyptus.

"Here's a napkin."

Her gaze on the low-roofed structures, she reached for the paper square. A slight tug-of-war brought her glance swinging back.

The doc had stuck another slip of paper inside the napkin. Only a corner of it protruded, but it was enough to start Taylor's heart tripping as she carried it and her glass to the fan-shaped rattan chair.

Mark picked up on the sudden, electric charge in the air. His brows drawing together, he zinged Taylor a quick look before engaging his one-time colleague in conversation.

"So, Oscar, what do you think of us working together again?"

"I think it would be an incredible opportunity to expand our fields of endeavor."

The glasses came off again. Beads of sweat dotted the scientist's brow.

"Diederik is most interested in whether we could meld your research in the ability of the conscious mind to remotely influence behavior with my work in regenerative bionetics. He thinks…we hope…it might be possible for patients or their doctors to influence the acceptance or rejection of transplanted organs."

"An interesting theory."

"Yes, it is."

Evincing a lively interest in their conversation, Taylor eased the note from the napkin. When she glanced down, the words leaped out at her.

Van Deursen has someone in my daughter's home. He'll kill her and my grandson if I don't cooperate. Please, please warn her as soon as you get off the island!

Well, hell! There went any hope of commandeering a boat and whisking Oscar Hayes to safety this morning. Before she could extract him, she had to send in a team to secure his daughter and grandson.

Sliding the note back inside the napkin, Taylor crumpled both and looked up to find the doc watching her with an anxious plea in his pale eyes.

She dipped her chin. Message received.

# Chapter 11

"This is Chase. Come in, Powell."

Kneeling on the deck of the fiberglass dive boat, Taylor kept her back to shore and pretended to check out the scuba equipment they'd borrowed at the marina. The boat was bug free, but she couldn't discount the possibility of observation.

Although the day was still hazed over, the sun beat down on her back. Bev had raided the pool cabana for a bathing suit that would fit her guest. It was skimpier than Taylor would have preferred, so she'd covered it with one of Mark's T-shirts to keep from getting a burn.

Mark wore his cutoffs, which dipped low in the back as he hunkered beside her. With his deep tan, he wasn't worried about the sun.

Tikal nosed in beside them. The dog's presence made for a crowd in the small deck well, but Taylor had other matters on her mind besides wet, hairy fur while she waited for Sergeant Powell to respond.

"Go ahead, Captain."

"Patch me through to Colonel Albright, ASAP. And stay on the loop. You need to hear this."

"Will do."

They'd anchored about fifty yards from the reef, ostensibly to salvage what they could from the ocean's depths. The storm to the south was already stirring up swells that would make the dive a challenge. Taylor braced a hand against the boat's side as a choppy wave slapped against the hull.

"Albright." The colonel's gruff voice came through the phone. "What have you got?"

"Dr. Hayes says van Deursen has someone planted inside his daughter's home to ensure his cooperation. He's convinced they'll harm her or his grandson. I can't move him until we secure them."

The colonel reacted with his usual decisiveness. "Give us three hours. Are you someplace where I can contact you when it's done?"

"Yes, sir. I'll set my phone to receive so it will alert me to your signal."

When Albright signed off, Powell came back on. "I caught that. This op gets hairier by the minute."

"Tell me something I don't know," Taylor muttered.

"You still planning to bring the doc out by boat?"

She eyed the clouds piling up to the south, hoping they didn't turn dark and ugly in the next three hours.

"That's the plan."

"The constable and I will have a welcome flotilla waiting. By the way, I ran the medical check you requested on van Deursen. His health records are sealed tighter than his financials. I couldn't find any indication he's been treated for a serious illness in the past twelve months in this country. Still checking with our friends in Europe."

Taylor was disappointed but not surprised.

"I dug up some early stuff on his wife," Powell continued. "The usual childhood ailments—measles, chicken pox. Nothing significant until the trucker she ran off with laid into her. Bastard roughed her up so badly she ended up in intensive care. Report says she almost died before they found a blood donor with her type."

A sudden premonition raised the hairs on the back of Taylor's neck.

"She's got an Rh factor that puts her in an extremely select group," Powell reported. "Supposedly it only turns up in about one out of every two hundred thousand folks."

The puncture wound at the base of Bev's skull took on new and ominous significance. Taylor would bet everything she owned that van Deursen was milking his wife's blood to sustain his own life.

Her mind whirling, she signed off and briefed the man beside her. "My boss is going to secure Dr. Hayes's daughter and grandson. He estimates they'd need three hours."

As she had just moments ago, Mark scanned the billowing clouds on the horizon. "Three hours might cut things a little close."

"I know." Biting her lip, Taylor worked the

timing in her head. "Here's the revised plan. We kill those hours diving, as advertised. As soon as we get word Hayes's daughter and grandson are safe, we head in. We tell the guys at the marina we're taking a break for a late lunch but want to go out again this afternoon. Then we find the doc."

From that point things would get chancy.

"You'll hustle Oscar down to the cove. I'll go back to the marina, tell Yardley and his pals that I'm picking you up there. Before I depart, I'll disable the helo and the other boats."

"How?" Mark asked sharply.

Their eyes locked above the jumble of tanks and regulators.

"I spotted a gas pump midway down the pier. I'll say I need to top off the dive boat. In the process, I spill some gas. Not much. Just enough for a nice little oil slick."

"Jesus!" Disbelief sent his brows soaring. "Please don't tell me you intend to ignite the slick and blow the whole damn marina."

She didn't *intend* to. Not the whole marina, anyway. The memory of what her brother had endured was too raw to think about igniting a fiery conflagration.

"If I do it right, the fire should just take the boat slips and helipad. Unless you can think of a better way to make sure we're not pursued."

After a pregnant pause, he conceded the point. "No. But I'm not letting you play arsonist by yourself. Oscar can make his own way down to the cove."

"I need you with him to run interference."

"Tough. I'm going with you."

Her mouth set. "We have to make sure Hayes gets to the cove. He's the reason we're here."

"He may be why *you're* here. *You're* the only reason I'm involved in this insane enterprise."

They squared off over the scuba gear. Neither was prepared to give an inch. The dog sensed their tension and thrust between them, providing both a distraction and a potential solution.

"Tikal can escort Hayes." Mark knuckled the animal behind the ears. "If I give the word, he'll rip out the throat of anyone who gets in their way."

"I thought you said he wasn't into throat ripping!"

"When did I say that?"

"When he went for mine that first night."

"Oh." His stubborn expression lightened. "I might have understated the case somewhat."

With an indignant huff, Taylor mulled over his suggestion. The risky part, she conceded, would be disabling pursuit. She could certainly use Mark's help there. And if they bungled that, they'd be the ones under suspicion, not Oscar. He could always claim he was just doing them a favor by exercising their dog and had no idea what they were up to at the marina.

"Okay, we'll send Tikal with Hayes."

He accepted the concession with a curt nod.

"There's more," she informed him. "Powell told me both van Deursens have extremely rare blood types. Too rare for mere coincidence."

Mark gave a long, low whistle. "Well, now we know why he married her."

"And why she married him. How many millions do you suppose he's forking over to Bev to suck her blood?"

"You're assuming that's all he wants from her."

The image of the glistening red organ tucked into its synthetic nest slammed into her. "Good grief! You think that was Bev's pancreas we saw regenerating itself?"

"I think it might have originated with cells from her pancreas."

"But Hayes said the donor cells came from a cow."

"He also said they were years away from transplanting the regenerated organs into a human. It's obvious van Deursen doesn't have years."

So the doc had fed them the company line for the benefit of anyone listening in. A tight ball formed in the pit of Taylor's stomach as she considered the implications.

Oscar and company had already regenerated a liver, lungs and a pancreas. If van Deursen's disease progressed, he'd need a new heart. Kidneys. Bone marrow. God knew what else.

How much could they take out of Bev before her own internal systems shut down? And why the hell should Taylor care? The woman must have known the risks when she agreed to a marriage of convenience.

Except it didn't come across as a marriage of convenience. Not on Bev's side, at least. The more time Taylor spent with the effervescent Texan, the more convinced she was that Bev felt a genuine affection for her husband. Then again, several million in reparations for her internal organs might spawn a whole lot of liking.

"Sergeant Powell pegged it," Taylor muttered as she strapped on her tank and adjusted the harness. "This op gets hairier by the minute."

Switching mental gears, she watched Mark test the regulator on the second tank. "Tell me I wasn't stretching the truth when I told Yardley you know how to dive."

"You weren't stretching the truth."

Jogging, and now diving. The man had certainly expanded his interests since their University of Michigan days. Taylor tilted him an inquiring glance.

"When did you take up scuba?"

"A few years ago. A colleague and I spent a six-month sabbatical in Australia. We checked out the Great Barrier Reef."

He said it evenly, with no particular inflection, but she had to ask.

"Was this colleague male or female?"

"Female."

From the dossier Intelligence had put together, she knew he'd never been engaged or married. A need to know more about the man she'd recon-nected with after their disastrous beginning prompted another question.

"Six months in Australia? Sounds like you two were pretty close."

"We were."

"What happened?"

He measured her through the screen of his lashes for several moments before satisfying her curiosity.

"We had similar interests," he said slowly. "Compatible careers. But we didn't really communicate. Not the way you and I do."

"You couldn't get into her head?"

"I never tried."

Legs spread, he braced himself against the rock of the boat. His gaze held hers, level and steady.

"You're the only woman I seem to connect with that way, Taylor. Then, and now."

Well, hell! She wasn't prepared for that, or for the wry comment that followed.

"After last night, I'd say we connect pretty well at every level."

As if to prove his point, he hooked a finger in her tank harness and tugged her closer. The kiss was a little rough. He was still wound up over her plan to torch the marina. So was she, for that matter.

"What about you?" Mark asked when they separated, both breathing hard. "Anyone hovering in the background I'll have to deal with when we return to the real world?"

"No one special."

"Why not, if you don't mind me asking?"

She did. This was hardly the time or the place to discuss her on again, off again love life. Since she'd initiated the inquisition, however, she could hardly cut it off now. Shrugging, she snapped the buckle on the web belt attached to her harness.

"I've had a few close encounters of the romantic kind, but..."

"But?"

It was her turn to hesitate. She'd put Mark off last night by telling him they'd talk about the feelings they roused in each other after they departed van Deursen's island. Honesty, and the tension building to a near boil inside her, forced a different response.

"I guess it was the same for me as it was for you. I never really connected with them."

"Good to know. I'd keep that knife handy if I were you," he added with a nod toward the scabbard attached to Taylor's belt.

Blinking at the apparent non sequitur, she glanced down. The knife nested inside the scabbard was standard issue for divers. Sharp enough to cut entangling kelp or seaweed. Too small to do serious damage to anything more threatening than a puff-fish.

"Why?" Frowning, she glanced over her shoulder. The goons manning van Deursen's marina were out of sight, but not out of mind. "You think we might have visitors?"

"We did the last time we went into the water here. A good-sized Gray Nurse came by to check us out."

"Gray Nurse? As in shark?"

"Correct."

Taylor eyed the choppy waves cutting across the surface of the sea with somewhat diminished enthusiasm.

"He got the message last time," Mark said as he scooped up his fins. "He shouldn't bother us."

"You telegraphed a message?" Her voice rose just a little. "To a shark?"

"I might have also flapped my hands and made threatening gestures."

"To a *shark?*"

Nodding absently, he leaned over the side of the boat to scoop water into his face mask. "Tikal, you'd better stay. No need to tempt fate."

The dog whined at being denied a swim but hunkered down on his haunches.

"Good boy," Mark said before tightening his mask, inserting his mouthpiece and falling backward with both fins up. He splashed into the sea, leaving Taylor with the choice of doing the same or yielding the field to possible saw-toothed visitors. With a reluctance that went bone-deep, she tugged on her face mask.

They didn't encounter any sharks, for which Taylor was profoundly relieved. Nor did they find more than a few scattered remnants of the *Ocean Breeze*.

The stern had broken off and sunk mere yards from the reef. Weighted down by the engine, it tipped at a thirty-degree angle against a coral out-cropping. The rest of the hull must have smashed into smaller pieces and been carried on the tide. On their first dive, Taylor recovered several pieces of navigational equipment. Mark brought up a shoe and a waterlogged laptop.

After the second dive, they rested in the boat and counted the minutes. The waves had pro-gressed from choppy to restless and rolling. Taylor prayed they wouldn't get worse before their planned second outing this afternoon.

Tension was crawling up her neck when her communications device gave off a discreet hum. She snatched it up, her heart pounding. "Chase."

"It's done," her boss said tersely. "We have the daughter and grandson in a safe house. Their new housekeeper is in custody and being held incommunicado."

"Excellent. We'll proceed with the extraction. We should have the target out by sixteen hundred."

That gave them a little over two hours. Plenty of time, Taylor assured her jumpy alter ego.

"Don't make it any later than that," Albright barked. "You know about the weather."

"Yes, sir."

"I've put a rescue C-130 out of Panama on alert. He'll launch in the next twenty minutes and stand off your location unless and until you need him."

Between the rescue bird and Sergeant Powell's welcoming flotilla, they should make it back to St. Kitts safely enough. Once they got off the island, that is.

"Contact me when you're clear," Albright instructed.

"Yes, sir."

Slipping the radio back into her boat shoe, Taylor dragged in a deep breath and met Mark's narrow gaze.

"The good guys have Hayes's daughter and grandson in safekeeping. Now it's our turn."

When they tied up at the marina, Yardley tried to talk them out of going back out again.

"The sea is starting to get rough," he pointed out unnecessarily.

"Only on the surface," Taylor countered with blithe self-assurance. "And if the storm does veer this way, we need to retrieve what we can before it hits."

He eyed the meager yield from their morning dives and shrugged. "I'll send one of my men with you. He's an experienced diver. Just in case."

"If you think that's necessary."

"I do. Mr. van Deursen would hold me personally responsible if anything happened to his guests."

"We can always use an extra pair of eyes," Mark lied smoothly. "We'll grab a sandwich, let it settle and be back in an hour."

Tucking the waterlogged laptop under his arm,

he waited for Taylor to collect her gear. They left their harnesses, fins and regulators in the boat. Yardley promised to swap out their tanks.

"I hope he doesn't refuel the boat," Taylor muttered as she and Mark climbed to the house. The zigzagging stairs allowed her to keep a casual eye on the marina. To her relief, Yardley left the dive boat just where it was tied.

Bev was stretched out on a lounge chair at the pool. Her long legs were bare and glistening with oil, but she wore a filmy cover-up over her suit.

She could hide the bruise, but she couldn't quite hide her grimace of pain as she sat up. "Hey, you two. Did you salvage anything?"

"My laptop." Mark displayed the titanium case. "I'm hoping Diederik might have some whiz on his staff who can extract the data."

"I'm sure he does. Y'all ready for lunch? I'll ring the kitchen."

"Let us clean up a little first," Taylor said with a smile. "Will Diederik or Oscar be joining us?"

"Diederik will. Oscar's still in his suite. Poor baby. He was up so late, he's probably still asleep."

"We'll knock on his door and see if he wants lunch."

"I don't know." Bev chewed on her lower lip. "Maybe you should let him sleep. He looked ready to drop when I talked to him earlier."

He'd look scared out of his gourd when *they'd* talked to him. The possibility their hostess had helped put that fear in his eyes hardened Taylor's smile until it felt baked on. Wagging a hand, she breezed past the blonde.

"Back in ten."

Oscar was indeed in his suite. His face was even more haggard and drawn, and his eyes pleaded for a reassurance Taylor couldn't wait to deliver. Once again, Tikal provided the solution.

"Bev sent us to see if you want to have lunch. We have to clean up first. And hose off the dog. He stinks worse than we do. Why don't you come out on the terrace and have a smoke with us while we get the smell off him?"

Grabbing his pipe, tobacco pouch and lighter, Hayes accompanied them outside. Taylor nudged him toward a round table and chairs while Mark unwound the hose rolled around a decorative wrought-iron mount.

Oscar's hands shook as he tamped tobacco into the bowl. His eyes pleaded with Taylor for information, but she waited to provide it until a stream of water arced through the air. Tikal thought the hose Mark turned on him was great fun. Barking and leaping joyously, he did a one-eighty in midair to take the full brunt of the spray. His noisy antics won a strained smile from Hayes and gave Taylor the cover she needed.

"Keep smiling, Dr. Hayes, and listen closely. We don't have much time. Your daughter and grandson have been moved to a safe house."

Removing the pipe clamped between his teeth, he stammered in surprise. "How…? How did this happen? When I passed you that note, I thought you would contact her when you left the island."

"When I leave, you leave."

Confusion blanked his face. "Who are you?"

A wild leap by Tikal sent water flying in all directions. Taylor threw up an arm and ID'ed herself through the crook of her elbow.

"I'm with the Air Force Office of Special Investigations. I was sent here to find you and, if you concurred, bring you home."

"Can you? Take me home?"

She lowered her arm. "We're damn sure going to try."

The scientist's glance went to his former collaborator, but Taylor didn't waste time explaining Wolfson's role in the op.

"Here's how it's going to happen. After lunch, Mark and I will take a boat out for another dive. You'll volunteer to exercise the dog for us down at the cove. We pick you up there and make for St. Kitts."

"Van Deursen has high-speed boats. A helicopter. They'll come after us."

"We'll take care of the boats and chopper."

Torn between hope and doubt, he gripped the carved bowl of his pipe in a white-knuckled fist. "Have you told Beverly about this?"

"Bev? No!"

"You must. She needs to come with us. If she doesn't, she'll die."

"She's voluntarily donating whatever the hell you're taking from her. I doubt she'll…"

"You don't understand. She doesn't, either!" Desperation thickened Hayes's voice. "Van Deursen brought me here hoping I could grow the organs he needs from his wife's donor cells. But his illness has progressed too rapidly and damaged his heart. He can't wait any longer. This morning I heard him instruct his medical team to prepare to harvest everything he needs. Pancreas. Lungs. Heart."

"He's going to take Bev's *heart?*"

At Hayes's anxious nod, Taylor had to fight a wave of disgust so strong it threatened to choke her. She'd bumped up against some real slugs in her time, but van Deursen's cold-blooded plan to rip his wife's still-beating heart out of her chest put him in a class by himself.

Oscar was right. They had to warn Bev, and fast, then get the hell out of Dodge. Scooping his lighter off the table, she shoved it in her shorts pocket and shouted to the still cavorting twosome.

"Hey, you guys! Cut the water ballet. Bev's waiting on us for lunch."

## Chapter 12

When the three of them emerged onto the terrace, Beverly was seated at a wrought-iron table shaded by the white-pillared cabana.

"Y'all just missed Diederik," she announced. "He said to tell you the storm to the south of us is buildin' a real head of steam. We're gonna batten down the hatches 'n ride it out, but he knows you and Mark won't want to get stuck here indefinitely. He's gone to check with his pilot 'bout flying you out this afternoon." She pouted a little in disappointment. "Sure hate for y'all to leave, but it's probably best with Diederik off his feed like he is."

If they'd needed confirmation of her husband's plans, Bev had just handed it to them. Van Deursen wanted the outsiders off his island before he appropriated his wife's most vital organs.

Her jaw tight, Taylor wondered how he intended to explain Beverly's sudden demise or disappearance to the authorities. And what kind of hold did he have over the members of his medical team that would keep them silent? Fear? Greed? Or had he threatened their families as he had Oscar's?

"Y'all ready for lunch? I'll call the kitchen and…"

"We need to talk to you."

The blonde blinked at Taylor's grim tone. When she took in the intent, intense expressions of the two men, she immediately assumed the worst.

"Oh, God! You bumped into Diederik! He's havin' another spell!"

"No, he…"

She shoved back her chair with a force that sent it crashing.

"Where is he? In his office? On the way to the clinic?"

Her filmy cover-up billowing, she was already rushing toward the stairs when Mark stepped in front of her.

"Diederik's okay."

"Don't BS me! Tell me straight!"

"I am telling you straight. As far as we know, your husband's fine."

Her shoulders drooping, Bev dragged in a shuddering breath. If this was an act, Taylor thought, the woman was damned good at it.

"Then why...? What...?" She swiped her lips, collecting herself. "What'd y'all want to talk to me about so serious like?"

"The offer Diederik made Taylor and me. We've consulted with Oscar and are definitely interested, but want your take on it."

"Mine? Good Lord! I don't know nothing... Dammit!"

Still shaken, she broke off and corrected herself with an embarrassed laugh.

"I don't know *anything* 'bout the business end of things, but I'd be more 'n happy to talk to you. Have a seat and we can gab while we eat."

"Why don't we walk down to the beach? I think better on my feet."

A little startled by the request, Bev gave her platform sandals a doubtful glance but acceded to her guest's wishes.

She, Mark and Oscar headed across the flagstones. Taylor lagged behind. Every instinct she possessed told her they were fast running out of time. Despite Mark's objections to her going it alone, she had to get to the marina, like now!

"You go on down," she told him. "I'll head for the marina and bring the dive boat around to the cove. We might have time for one last dive before we ship out."

"We talked about that," Mark countered swiftly. "You'll need my help refueling the boat and loading the gear. We'll go to the marina together, after we talk to Bev."

"No sense wasting time. You go ahead. I'll meet you at the beach."

"Dammit, Taylor…"

With a lightninglike mental gyration, she yanked the lock on the garden gate and threw open the portal.

*We've flat run out of time! We have to separate and move fast.*

*The hell we do!*

Smiling, she wagged her fingers in a casual farewell.

*Take Bev and the doc to the beach. Tell her what van Deursen plans. If I need you, I'll shout.*

Allowing him no further headspace for argument, she slammed the gate. "See you guys in a few minutes."

Mark stood planted to the flagstones. His head told him Taylor was right. Explaining the situation to Bev and escorting Oscar to the cove would eat precious time they didn't have. His gut told him just the opposite.

The decision came fast and sure. He'd let Taylor storm out and disappear from his life eight years ago. He couldn't—*wouldn't*—do it again.

Whirling, he took Bev's elbow in a tight grip and hustled her toward the path leading to the cove.

"You need to slow it down a tad," she said with a rueful smile. "Or at least let me kick off these clodhoppers."

Ignoring her protest, he propelled her into the lush green tunnel. He didn't spot the glint of security cameras but knew they scanned the path, as they did every other inch of the island.

They could watch. Hopefully they couldn't hear. Feigning a stumble, Mark knocked into Bev.

"Hey!"

She pitched forward on her platforms and would have fallen if not for his bruising grip on her elbow. He let her sag to her knees and knelt down beside her.

With a rueful grimace, she used her free hand to shove back her hair. "Better watch where you're steppin' there, doc."

Mark dug his fingers almost to the bone to keep her from rising. "Listen to me! Taylor's an air force undercover agent. She and I are taking Oscar off this island."

"Wh…? What?"

"Oscar isn't here voluntarily. I think you know that."

Guilt riddled her face. "Diederik's gonna make it up to him. Oscar will be a very rich man soon's Diederik gets well."

"He's not going to get well without desperate measures. You know that."

Mark made a show of dusting her off as he helped her to her feet. She needed his assistance. Shock and trepidation had turned her stark-white under her tan. She looked like she might collapse again at any minute.

"How soon after you married him did he ask you for donor cells, Bev?"

"It ain't like that. When I found out he was sick, I told him right off I'd give him whatever he needs. One of my kidneys. A slice of my liver."

"Your heart and lungs?"

The color leached from her face. "My heart?"

"He's going to take them. As soon as he shuffles Taylor and me off the island."

"You're lying," she croaked hoarsely. "You gotta be lying."

"I wish I was. Diederik threatened to kill Oscar's daughter and grandson if he didn't cooperate. He'll kill you, too, to save himself."

"He wouldn't!" Desperation made her accent as thick as Brazos River mud. "He's teachin' me how to talk right, buyin' me all those beautiful clothes to show me off when he's well. He wouldn't take my heart."

Despite her frantic denial, disbelief warred with a sick uncertainty in her eyes when she twisted around to Oscar.

"Would he?"

Perspiration sheened the scientist's face as he nodded grimly.

Bev gave a small moan, and Mark didn't wait for more. Shoving her forward, he transferred his grip on her elbow to Oscar.

"Take her down to the beach. I'll meet you there. Tikal!"

The animal lifted his head.

"Go with them."

*And guard them.*

Mark figured he had five, maybe ten, minutes until someone questioned the unusual movements by van Deursen's wife and guests. Retracing his steps, he crossed the terrace, found the path leading to the marina stairs and broke into a run.

Relief swept through Taylor as she stepped out onto the dock. The dive boat was tied right where they'd left it.

The wind had picked up considerably. Her hair whipped, stinging her cheeks as she shoved a hand in her shorts pocket and gripped Oscar's lighter in a tight fist. Pasting on a smile, she breezed past the guard who'd given her and Mark the guided tour earlier. He and one of his pals were busy muscling wave runners out of the water and onto a trailer hitched to a small tractor.

"Change of plans," she said cheerfully. "I'm taking the dive boat around to the beach to pick up Dr. Wolfson."

"Wait, Ms. Chase!" Scrambling onto the pier, the guard came after her. "Mr. van Deursen called down a while ago. He said you and Dr. Wolfson are flying out this afternoon ahead of the storm."

She nodded. "We are, but not before we get in one last dive. Did you top off the gas in the boat?"

The guard hesitated, unsure of his orders in this situation. "Not yet, but you'd better let me check with Yardley before you take off."

"No problem. I'll fill her up while you talk to your boss."

Her heart spurting pure adrenaline, she untied the dive boat. The empty craft rode high in the water and pulled easily toward the pump a dozen yards away.

At the end of the pier, well clear of the boat-house, the sleek JetRanger III sat on the helipad. Below the pad, waves washed in, rushed out, each swell cutting a foamy path through the pilings.

Taylor secured the dive boat and clambered

into the deck well. Her hand shook as she reached for the pump handle. Instead of opening the engine cowling and inserting the nozzle into the fuel tank, however, she filled the spare gas can stowed below the rear seat. Her palms swam with sweat as she gripped the squeeze bar.

If she didn't get this right, if she misjudged the ebb and flow of those swirling waves, the oil slick could engulf her boat right along with the chopper and the other boats still sitting in their slips.

That possibility weighed almost as heavily as the searing memory of what her brother endured. She intended to make damn sure everyone at the marina knew what would happen before she ignited the slick.

Steeling herself, she cut off the pump, loosened the tie down and shoved away from the dock. She was scrambling back into the deck well just as Alex Yardley strode out of the Ops Center. Above his black T-shirt, his heavy features were set in a scowl.

"I'm sorry, Ms. Chase." His island lilt carried a steely edge. "Please tie up again. Mr. van Deursen issued specific instructions."

"I know. He thinks we should depart the island ahead of the storm." She pushed the starter button.

Once. Twice. "We want to get in another quick dive first."

"Not possible." He hooked an impatient arm. "Please, bring the boat back in."

She hit the starter again, and the engine sputtered to life. Shoving the throttle forward, she spun the wheel. The boat bucked, leveled out and angled away from the dock.

"Ms. Chase!"

His boots pounded the dock as he kept pace with her, or tried to.

The slips whizzed by. Yardley broke into a run. He couldn't figure out why she was heading in toward shore instead of out to sea but he was fast realizing she had something other than an afternoon dive in mind.

He still hadn't figured out what when she spun the wheel again and aimed back the way she'd just come. Anchoring the wheel with one hand, she dragged out the spare gas can with the other.

The gasoline spewed out. Yardley gave a savage shout that brought his men running. Taylor shoved the throttle to full speed, and laid a glistening trail back along the slips.

The first shot went high over her head.

The second spit into the water twenty yards ahead.

They wouldn't risk hitting the boat itself. They couldn't! If it blew, it might take the whole marina with it. That was her rationale, anyway, as she crouched low in the deck well and sped past the pump.

The next shot shattered both the windshield and her misplaced confidence in the collective smarts of van Deursen's black-shirted thugs.

Another thirty yards to the helipad. Fifteen. Five.

Over her jackhammering heart, she could hear the thunder of running feet. Bullets buzzed into the sea all around her, soundless splats that looked like pellets hitting the water.

Finally! The helipad!

Still splashing gas, she yanked on the wheel and cut around the end of the dock. So close the hull grazed the pilings supporting the pad. So fast, she almost lost control of her speeding craft.

It rocked wildly and tried to buck Taylor into the sea, but she held on and gained a few precious seconds before Yardley and company charged to this side of the dock.

Tossing the gas can overboard, she yanked the throttle to Neutral and grabbed the hem of her T-shirt. A swift tug had it up and over her head. She wadded it into a ball, leaving only a small tail, and thrust a hand in her shorts pocket for the lighter she'd appropriated from Oscar's suite.

One click ignited a blue flame. Taylor held it to the dangling tail. The white cotton turned brown, then a bright glowing red. The fire took hold just as Yardley and his men burst into view on the near side of the pier.

"Jesus!"

The startled exclamation carried clearly across the stretch of water separating her from them.

"She's gonna blow the whole friggin' place!"

Taylor looked up, locked glances with Yardley and tossed the now flaming T-shirt into the slick a few yards from her drifting boat.

A line of bright orange lit up on the surface of the water. Zinging toward the dock, it stampeded the men who'd stood gaping in frozen disbelief a moment before. Shouting and cursing, they ran like hell.

All but one.

His face suffused with fury, Alex Yardley

whipped up his weapon and gripped it in both hands, police-style. Through the black smoke now rising from the burning gasoline, Taylor saw him widen his stance and take a deliberate bead.

She dived for the throttle. Braced for the impact of a bullet slamming in between her shoulder blades at any second, she heard a furious shout.

"Hey! Turn around, you bastard!"

For a confused millisecond, Taylor thought Mark was in her head. Then the unmistakable thunder of pounding feet twisted her around. Squinting through the billowing smoke, she saw him charge straight for Yardley.

The gun in the guard's hand kicked. Mark jerked, faltered and forged ahead. Taylor's heart stop dead in her chest.

"No!"

The scream ripped from her even as momentum carried Mark into Yardley. Both men went down.

The glistening trail Taylor had laid was fully ignited now. Flames circled the helipad, licking at the pilings, and raced along the side of the pier housing the boat slips. The toxic stink of scorched fiberglass added to the stench of burning gasoline.

The ski boats and wave runners still rocking in the slips could go at any second.

Taylor barely registered the suffocating danger. Her whole being was centered on the two men locked together, rolling and pounding on each other. Wrenching the wheel, she aimed for the side of the pier not yet engulfed by flames. She couldn't breathe for the fumes and the fear that clogged her throat when she saw Mark plow his fist into Yardley's face.

Tearing the weapon from the man's slack hand, Mark staggered to his feet. A bright red splotch sprouted amid the gaudy green of his tropical shirt. More blood poured from his nose, which must have taken a direct hit from Yardley's fist.

"Here!" she screamed through the curtain of smoke. "Over here!"

Dazed, he didn't seem to hear her. Either the wound or the smoke had confused him. He lurched toward burning slips.

Racked with terror, Taylor ripped open the portal. *Mark! Turn around.*

*Taylor?*

*I'm here! Turn around. Please! Please! Come to me!*

Spinning, he stumbled in her direction just as Yardley pushed to his feet. The burly guard took one step toward him, but changed his mind about continuing the battle when he spotted the flames leaping up from the boat slips. He took off running, and Mark dived in.

He surfaced some twenty yards from Taylor. Eyes burning from the smoke, she brought the boat around and threw herself half over the side to grab his arm.

Hacking, coughing, grunting, sobbing with the effort, she dragged him aboard. He collapsed in the deck well, grimy from the smoke and drenched in seawater that tinted a pale, bloody pink almost before he hit the deck.

The vicious little hole in his shirt welled with fresh blood, but Taylor couldn't take the precious seconds to stanch it. Scrambling forward, she hit the throttle again.

The dive boat was constructed for sturdiness and convenience, not speed, and maxed out at sixteen knots. She pushed it to the limit and zoomed away from the marina.

They were maybe a hundred yards out when the first boat went up with an ear-popping boom.

Another exploded a half second later. Taylor wrenched around in time to see the pilings supporting the helipad crumple. The gleaming red and white JetRanger with the distinctive DvD logo on its fuselage slid slowly, ponderously, into the sea.

Then the flames danced up the pilings beneath the fuel pump at middock. Taylor had no more than a heartbeat to throw herself atop Mark before the storage tank that fed the pump went up with a deafening roar, taking the boathouse, van Deursen's multimillion dollar yacht and the rest of the dock with it.

# Chapter 13

Debris rained down in huge, clanking pieces and smaller, flaming chunks. Only a scattered few came anywhere near the dive boat.

"Tay-lor."

With her ears still ringing from the percussive boom, she almost missed the low grunt.

"Mark?"

Levering herself off his slumped body, she scrambled onto her knees. His eyes were open and the pupils focused, thank God, although his lips had pulled back in a rictus of pain.

"Don't move. You took a bullet."

"Yeah." Ignoring her advice, he struggled to sit up. "I...figured that...out."

The reply had her teetering between relief and near hysteria. "If you can manage sarcasm, you must not hurt too badly."

"Wanna bet?"

She helped him prop his shoulders against the side of the boat and peeled back his gaudy tropical shirt. The wound was in the right side of his chest, close to his armpit. The emergency first-aid training she'd received as a rookie hardly qualified her as an EMT. But he wasn't dribbling or coughing up blood so she let herself hope the bullet had passed through muscle without nicking his ribs or lungs.

"Lean on me," she bit out. "I need to check for an exit wound."

Yep, there it was. Small and round and oozing.

With a prayer of thanks that the bullet hadn't fragmented on impact and done more damage, Taylor gave him the news. "You've got two holes, one front, one back. I'm going to do a quick patch job, then we'll go after Oscar, Bev and Tikal."

"I'm okay," he insisted gruffly. "Just go."

"And have you bleed all over the deck? I don't think so."

All boats carried first-aid kits. Taylor rooted through the deck lockers until she found what she needed. Swiping the grime and smoke from her hands as best she could, she dusted antiseptic powder on a folded gauze pad and pressed it to the entry wound.

"Hold this."

Guiding his good arm to the pad, she had him lean forward again. Another pad went over the exit wound. She wrapped both with a roll of cotton gauze and checked his pupils again to make sure he hadn't gone into shock.

"I'm okay," he insisted again, his voice stronger and more impatient. "Go."

"Could be a bumpy ride," she warned.

"I'll manage. Help me up onto that... Good Lord!"

Jaw slack, he got his first full view of the billowing clouds of black smoke and the flames leaping from what was left of the marina.

His face angled toward hers. Admiration and a hint of rueful laughter crept into eyes rimmed red from the smoke. "Remind me to think twice before turning you loose with a cigarette lighter."

Only then did she realize how much she loved this man.

Stark terror had iced her veins when he'd charged Yardley. Suffocating fear had gripped her by the throat after the gun went off. She hadn't pulled in a whole breath until she'd dragged him aboard and checked out his wound.

But now he sat there with his hair dripping wet and his face streaked with grime, making light of what was still an iffy situation.

"If you're going to do something," she said, emotion rolling through her like an Abrams tank, "you might as well do it right."

She would have said more if a flutter of movement at the top of the stairs hadn't snagged her attention.

"Uh-oh. Van Deursen's army is about to descend. Time to depart the scene."

They circled around the remains of the marina to avoid floating debris. Once clear, Taylor set a straight course for the jutting promontory that protected van Deursen's private beach. En route, she wrestled the radio out of her shoe and told Sergeant Powell to launch the welcome flotilla.

She spotted Oscar and Bev as soon as the dive boat rounded the sheer rock precipice. Oscar was on his feet. His back and shoulders rigid, he squinted at the boat cutting toward him, obviously trying to determine who was aboard.

Bev sat in the sand. She'd drawn up her knees and buried her face in her crossed arms. Her utter desolation might have stirred a tug of sympathy if Taylor had emotion to spare.

When they drew near shore, she cut the engine and let the boat ride on the swells. Oscar splashed into the surf and met it halfway in.

"We heard an explosion!"

"There was a slight accident at the marina."

"Diederik?" Bev lifted a tear-streaked face. "Is he…?"

"He wasn't there."

Her shoulders slumped. "Thank God."

Taylor swung the boat around in the knee-deep surf. She couldn't go in any closer or she'd ground it. "Climb aboard, Oscar."

The scientist tried twice to swing his leg over the side. Taylor abandoned the wheel and plunged over the side to give him a boost. Gritting his teeth, Mark reached down with his good arm and hauled the man in by the collar.

"Where's Tikal?"

"He was here, with us." Oscar shoved his glasses up on the bridge of his nose and searched the bushy palmettos fringing the cove. "He must have heard a bird or a mouse and gone to investigate."

Mark's shrill whistle pierced the air only a few inches from Taylor's ear. Wincing, she called to the blonde on the beach.

"Com'on, Bev." Hanging onto the side of the boat, she fought to keep it steady in the foaming surf. "We gotta go."

Slowly Bev pushed to her feet. Her broken dreams weighting her down, she took a hesitant step.

Another high-pitched whistle had Taylor hunching her shoulders.

"Move it, Bev! We have to…"

She broke off with a muttered awshit as the sound of engines revving penetrated the cove. Small vehicles, her brain registered. Most likely ATVs. Coming downhill. Fast.

The military officer in Taylor said to clamber aboard and lay on all speed. She had Oscar in the boat. He was her objective, the sole reason she'd crashed van Deursen's private party. She'd be crazy to risk losing him for an animal that was more wolf than dog and a woman who'd known all along Hayes was here under duress.

"You hear those vehicles, Bev? One of them is sure to hold Diederik. He wants your heart and lungs and anything else he can tear out of you. Are you going to give them to him?"

Stricken, the blonde waded into the surf. Her cover-up floated around her calves. The unmistakable sound of ATVs changing gears stopped her in her tracks.

Taylor spit out a curse and bunched her muscles. She was all set to drag the woman into the boat by her hair when the palmettos parted.

Well, hell! She'd guessed right. Diederik van Deursen occupied the passenger seat of the vehicle that roared onto the beach. What looked like half of his goon squad followed.

The lead ATV lurched to a halt at water's edge. The others fanned out on either side. Taylor sucked in a swift breath as the occupants displayed enough semiautomatics to equip a medium-size dictatorship.

"They won't shoot her," Mark predicted grimly.

"They can't. Organs have to be harvested from living donors."

"That doesn't mean they won't shoot us!"

To her profound relief, van Deursen seemed more inclined to persuasion at that moment than firepower.

"Beverly. Darling."

Descending from the lead ATV, he stretched out an imploring hand. "Don't believe the lie these people have told you."

"Which lie?" Bev stood midcalf in the surf, tears rolling down her cheeks. "That you never loved me? That you married me only 'cause we have the same blood type? That you want me to give you more 'n just a few donor cells?"

In Taylor's biased opinion, van Deursen gave the performance of his life. His face pale and anguished, he pleaded with his wife.

"All right. I admit I searched the blood database until I found a perfect match. I admit I came to L.A. with the specific intent of luring you to my island. I never thought, I never dreamed, I would fall in love with you. Please, my darling. Please come back to me."

"Don't do it, Bev!" Taylor couldn't restrain

herself. "He doesn't want you. He wants the weeks or months or years you can give him. Problem is, you have to die to do it."

A small, animal moan issued from the blonde. "I never had a life until he married me. Maybe... Maybe it's only fair I give back what I got."

"No!"

"Yes, my darling. Yes." Van Deursen stretched out his arm. "Come to me."

He stepped forward. Taylor tensed. Behind her, Mark planted a hand on the side of the boat, ready to jump over. Oscar froze them all in place.

"She won't save you, Diederik. She can't."

Van Deursen's eyes narrowed to slits. "What are you talking about?"

"You thought you could terrorize me into going along with your sick plans. You thought you could hold the lives of my daughter and my grandson ransom." The scientist erupted with pent-up fury. "I didn't *take* cells from Bev last night. I *injected* her."

"With what?"

"A combination of chemicals used to treat cancer. The cocktail kills red blood cells, leaving only the white to fight infection. Her organs need those red blood cells to function, Diederik, and her body needs time to manufacture them. Until it does, her heart and lungs will do you no good."

"I don't believe you!"

"No?" Whipping off his glasses, Oscar jabbed them toward Bev. "Why do you think she's so pale? Why has she felt so miserable today?"

Taylor figured her misery might have something to do with the fact that her husband wanted to dice her up. She didn't say a word, however, as the drama played out, second by agonizing second.

It ended when Diederik broke. After agonizing moments of doubt and indecision, he plunged into the surf.

"It's not too late! It can't be too late!"

Taylor and Mark lunged for Bev, but van Deursen reached his wife first. He locked his fist around her upper arm with a bruising force that elicited a cry of pain and dragged her toward shore.

As if waiting for just that signal, a blur of silver and gray burst out of the palmettos. Tikal streaked through the line of ATVs. Before van Deursen's goon squad could react, he went for van Deursen's throat.

Man and dog went under, dragging Bev with them. Hands slapped and metal snicked as van Deursen's army chambered rounds. None of the black-shirted guards fired, though. They couldn't for fear of hitting their boss.

Taylor and Mark were still lunging toward Bev when she shot out of the swells. Gasping, she floundered and thrashed around until she found her footing.

"Oh, God, oh, God, oh, God!"

Her frantic hands locked on to her husband's arm and dragged him up. Taylor expected to see savaged throat muscle or glistening vocal cords. There were fang marks to be sure, but no raw flesh.

Tikal shot up beside Bev a second later and snarled a warning that van Deursen was beyond hearing. Clutching his chest with both hands, the billionaire gasped his wife's name.

"Beverly…"

His damaged heart gave out before the last syllable passed through his lips. His eyes rolled back in his head. His breath left on a sigh. Still clutching his chest, he sank below the surface once more.

Both Mark and Taylor went to his aid, but they

knew before they helped a frantic Bev drag him up it was too late. No amount of CPR would revive the man. Still, someone had to try. Taylor decided to leave it up to the goons who had run forward.

"Any of you know CPR!"

Two of the uniformed men stretched van Deursen out on the sand and pumped his chest. Bev sank to the sand beside them. When they gave up the effort, a long-drawn-out wail tore from the back of her throat.

"Deeeederik!"

What happened next was right out of a spaghetti Western. Leaderless, van Deursen's men couldn't decide what they were supposed to do now—until one idiot mumbled something and raised his weapon. The rest followed suit. In the blink of an eye, a semicircle of cocked weapons was aimed at Taylor and Mark.

"Whoa," Taylor said, palms up. "Take it easy, boys."

If anything, that seemed to kick the tension up another notch. One of the men said something in a thick, local dialect she couldn't understand. Another reached for the radio clipped to his belt.

Uh-oh. If he was contacting Yardley, matters

could get real nasty, real fast. Her palms still spread, Taylor opened the gate and sent an urgent communiqué.

*Hey! Wolfson!*

His chin jerked. His glance sliced in her direction.

*Thought you should know I love you.*

*What?*

She had to smile at the look on his face. *Well?*

*Didn't I say it?*

*Not in so many words.*

He let loose with an oath Taylor would bet few Princeton professors had ever uttered but followed it with what she wanted to hear.

*I love you, too.*

*Good to know.*

*Any ideas how to end this stand-off?*

*I'm thinking.*

To their combined astonishment, it was Bev who defused the situation. Cradling her husband's body in her arms, she gave a broken sob.

"Put down your guns," she told the guards. "I won't have no shooting or killing."

In the taut silence that followed, Taylor hoped

she'd been right in thinking van Deursen ruled his private kingdom through greed or fear.

Now that he was dead, his employees had no reason to fear him…and every reason to obey the orders of his very young, very wealthy widow.

Her supposition proved to be true when they lowered their weapons. Just to be sure, though, Taylor extracted her phone and contacted Sergeant Powell.

"This is Captain Chase." She pitched her voice loud enough to make sure the squad heard every word. "Mr. van Deursen has just suffered an apparent heart attack. He's dead. I need you, Constable Benjamin and the rest of the contingent from St. Kitts to proceed to van Deursen's island ASAP."

After receiving an acknowledgment from Powell, she snapped the phone shut.

"The police are on their way. Let's load the body in an ATV and take it up to the clinic."

The remains of the marina were still smoldering when the contingent from St. Kitts arrived. Mark, Taylor and Oscar parted company with Bev an hour later.

Constable Benjamin and two of his men

would remain on the island with her. More police inspectors were already en route from Basseterre. In addition, a medical investigation team was being assembled to assess the operation of the research lab and the clinic. Bev would have plenty of company while she explained her role in the organ regeneration process to the investigators.

Ravaged by grief and a loneliness that looked like it cut to the bone, the Texan came out on the terrace to say goodbye.

"I didn't know Diederik threatened your daughter 'n grandson. I'm real sorry for that."

The scientist merely nodded.

"You 'n Sulim 'n the others did good work here, some real valuable research. Maybe… Maybe when this is over, you kin pick it up again, here or wherever suits you. Far as I know, I'm Diederik's sole beneficiary. I'll see you get whatever dollars you need."

The promise of unlimited funding produced more tangible results than Bev's apology. Unbending, Oscar promised to consider her offer.

She extended one to Mark, as well. "Diederik wanted you on his team. I'm not real sure what he'd promised you, but I'll honor it." Her mouth twisted in a wry smile. "I may have to take care of all this from jail, but I'll see it gets done."

Taylor bet she would, too. The woman didn't lack for loyalty or guts. Driven by a reluctant concern, she made a suggestion.

"If you want, I'll talk to Constable Benjamin about letting you go back to Basseterre with us. You can talk to the authorities there."

"I'll stay."

"You need to get off this island. Especially if that storm hits, which is looking more likely by the minute."

"I can't leave. I gotta take care of Diederik."

"Why?"

The blunt question drew a sad smile. "He took care of me when I was down and out."

"He did it for his own reasons."

"I know, but I think…I'm sure…he loved me. A little."

Taylor gave up. Clearly the woman wanted to cling to her illusions.

"You have my card. You know how to reach me if you need to."

# Chapter 14

The trip back to St. Kitts's capital was one Taylor decided she'd rather forget.

Although Tropical Storm Gail was still more than sixty miles to the south, her winds had churned twelve- to fourteen-foot swells. Both Taylor and Tikal heaved up their breakfast. By the time Mark got them off the boat and onto dry land, the old cliché about being as sick as a dog had taken on a whole new meaning.

Given Oscar's enforced incarceration by van Deursen, the St. Kitts's chief police inspector agreed to let him dictate a detailed statement and depart for home ahead of the storm. While he provided his statement, Taylor contacted her boss's exec and left a brief message for the colonel.

"Mission accomplished. Dr. Hayes will be on his way home tonight. Van Deursen suffered a massive heart attack and died prior to the extraction. More detailed report to follow."

Taylor, Mark and Sergeant Powell put Oscar on the last plane out before the airport shut down. She also arranged for a counterpart to meet him upon arrival and unite him with his daughter and grandson.

Powell left on the same plane. His part of the op was over. With an overnight layover in Miami, the communications tech would reach his duty station in North Carolina midafternoon tomorrow. Taylor and Mark, on the other hand, would remain in St Kitts for the next few days to tie up the op's loose ends.

All too conscious of Mark's bloody shirt, Taylor insisted they leave Tikal in the care of an obliging constable and make a trip to Basseterre's big, modern hospital. Although his wound had been cleaned and dressed by van Deursen's medical staff and Mark swore he wasn't hurting too badly, they were both relieved when X-rays confirmed the bullet hadn't cracked a rib or done serious tissue damage.

"I'm going to give you some painkillers," the E.R. doc said as she surveyed her patient.

Mark was still in his cutoffs and bloodstained tropical shirt. His eyes showed more red than white, and grime had collected at the corners. Combined with the five o'clock shadow darkening his cheeks and chin, he looked like someone you didn't want to bump into in a dark alley.

Taylor knew she didn't look much better. She'd changed into the borrowed drawstring slacks and a clean blouse before departing van Deursen's island, but her hair was still spiked with salt water and oily smoke had penetrated every one of her pores.

"You may not ache much now," the doc told him, "but you will in the morning. I suggest you take two before you go to bed tonight."

"Speaking of beds," Mark commented when he and Taylor emerged into a swiftly descending night punctuated by driving wind and torrential rain. "Do we have one?"

"We do. The chief inspector's assistant fixed us up while Oscar was dictating his statement."

They ducked into a taxi for the short ride back to police headquarters. Taylor held the cab while Mark reclaimed his dog, then they wound through rain-soaked streets to the hotel perched high on a hill overlooking the harbor.

Truth be told, Taylor didn't have the slightest objection to riding out the storm in Basseterre—especially in a low-rise, colonial-style building constructed with granite blocks mined from a local quarry. The desk clerk assured them the establishment had survived a good half dozen hurricanes. A mere tropical storm presented no real threat. Just to be safe, they should close and securely latch the plantation shutters leading to their second-story balcony. They might also want to fill the tub and check out the hurricane lamp in their room in case the hotel lost power and/or drinking water.

Once inside the airy, comfortable room, Taylor admitted her willingness to remain in Basseterre had a whole lot less to do with wrapping up the loose ends of her op than the prickly sense of anticipation that had been building in her since they'd put Oscar on the plane. She couldn't wait to shower away her residual grime and slide between clean white sheets beside Mark—*without* having to control her movements or swallow her groans of delight.

She'd be gentle, she vowed. She'd have to, given his wound. She'd also make sure he popped a couple of the pills the E.R. doc had given him to minimize the pain and maximize the pleasure. First, though, she had to feed both man and beast.

"We'd better call down to room service and get in an order before the kitchen closes. What are you hungry for?"

"Conch stew, fire grilled shrimp and you. Not necessarily in that order."

Taylor grinned at the prompt reply, thrilled that their thoughts were running along similar lines.

Unless…

"You weren't just mucking around inside my head, were you?"

"No. Why?" A smile worked its way into his smoke-reddened eyes. "Were you thinking about cool sheets and hot sex, too?"

"As a matter of fact, I was."

"Make that phone call." Popping the buttons of

his shirt with his good hand, he headed for the bathroom. "We'll need sustenance, and lots of it, for what I have in mind."

Despite his bravado, Mark was operating on sheer willpower. The right side of his chest ached like a sunnuvabitch and the smoke he'd swallowed made his lungs feel like they were spiked with broken glass. Grimacing, he fished out the pain-killers and downed two before shedding his clothes.

The E.R. doc had resealed the wounds with plastic, waterproof bandages, thank God. Mark wanted a hot, pounding shower almost as much as he wanted to stretch out beside Taylor in that king-size bed. Almost.

By the time he'd steamed up the small bathroom, the scales had tipped far more toward the woman waiting her turn in the tub. She greeted him with a towel and assurances that dinner was on its way.

"You okay?" she asked, skimming a glance over his patched chest.

It still ached, but the pills were starting to kick in. Hitching the towel around his waist, Mark nodded. "Feeling better by the second. Want me to scrub your back?"

There was hardly room to turn around in the bathroom, let alone in the shower/tub combination. Taylor declined the offer with a smile that promised better things to come.

"Dinner should be here any minute. I ordered two rare filet mignons for Tikal, by the way. I figure he deserves a reward for taking van Deursen down."

Mark hooked a brow. "And precipitating a fatal heart attack?"

"If you ask me, the bastard got off easy."

The pelting water washed away both the grit and the weariness that had crept over Taylor while she'd waited for Mark to finish. Her skin flushed and her body tingling, she wrapped a towel around her and raked her fingers through her shampooed hair.

Too late, she realized they should have stopped for a few essentials before holing up in the hotel. Like toothbrushes and disposable razors and clean underwear. Tomorrow, she vowed. Assuming the streets weren't inundated. For now she'd have to make do with hand-washing the thong panties she was starting to get used to. Mindful of the desk clerk's instructions, she also scrubbed out the tub and ran it full of clean water before joining the two males in the other room.

Both were sound asleep.

Tikal had wolfed down his dinner. The two plates on the floor were licked clean. A soup bowl filled with water sat beside them. More dishes topped with aluminum covers were stacked on a tray on a side table. The dog lay on his side close to Mark's chair. One of his rear legs was hiked in the air, twitching and pawing.

Mark was sprawled in the room's only chair, his legs outstretched and his ankles crossed on the coffee table. The towel he'd wrapped around his waist had slipped to reveal the swirl of dark hair around his navel.

Taylor's pulse tripped, but the lines of weariness etched into his face put a kink in the plans she'd formulated for the night.

He looked so tame like this, she thought ruefully. His head resting against the back of the chair and his eyes closed. His muscles were relaxed and loose. His elbows draped over the arms of the chair. When a small snore issued from his parted lips, she grinned and abandoned the last of her lascivious intentions.

The hammer of rain on the roof drowned out her footsteps as she dragged the spread from the bed. Padding back to the chair, she settled it lightly over Mark and bent to brush her lips over his.

*Sleep well. Both of you,* she added with an amused glance at the still twitching Tikal.

She wasn't prepared for the hand that shot out and locked around her wrist. Or for lazy heat that lit Mark's eyes when his lids lifted.

"Sleep, hell."

"Dammit!" She couldn't decide whether to laugh or pout in exasperation. "I didn't open any portals. How did you hear me?"

"ESP. Remote sensing. Sheer, unadulterated lust. Take your pick."

His tug on her wrist urged her to hook a leg over his and straddle his lap. As much as she wanted to do just that, Taylor resisted.

"You're exhausted. And wounded. Judging by your pupils, you're also flying a little high at the moment."

"Not too high to pleasure my woman."

"Your woman?" That brought a little rush of heat and a sputter of indignant laughter. "You're regressing, Professor Wolfson. Must be the pills. This is the twenty-first century, not the seventeenth."

"Works the same in any century." With a slow, predatory grin, he tugged on her wrist again. "You'll have to do most of the work, but I'll hold up my end of the deal."

Since that was pretty much what Taylor had decided earlier, she could hardly object. Especially when his end of the deal had already produced a noticeable peak in the towel draped over his lap.

Still, she proceeded with extreme caution. Discarding both towels, she nudged his leg aside and sank to her knees in the cradle of his thighs.

"How about I pleasure my man first?"

She took the hard, hot length of him in a loose grip and raked the tip of one nail along the pulsing vein. He sucked in a sharp breath. And let it out again on a hiss when she leaned in and licked the engorged tip.

"Taylor! Don't forget you're dealing with a somewhat incapacitated man here."

"He doesn't look incapacitated from my perspective. Relax," she said with a wicked grin. "This won't hurt too much."

She licked him again, deriving a fierce, feminine satisfaction from his inarticulate grunt. Moments later she took him in her mouth.

Mark stood the exquisite torture longer than Taylor thought he could. But his eyes were dark with desire when he fisted his hands in her hair and dragged her head up for a kiss that left them both greedy for more.

"Bed," Taylor panted. "Flat. Now."

The sheets were cool and soft and smelled of sunshine, a perfect contrast to the rain lashing at the shuttered windows. The wind howled like the dogs of hell as Taylor straddled Mark's thighs and eased down slowly, so slowly.

She levered upward every bit as slowly. He gripped her hips to anchor her but let her set the pace. Taylor wasn't sure whether it was mere moments or hours before she felt the heat building in her belly. She squeezed her muscles, determined to take him with her. His sudden stiffening told her she'd succeeded.

Her head went back. Her neck arched. Gloriously uninhibited and free of all fear of surveillance, she didn't even try to hold back her moan when she climaxed.

The wind was still howling when they woke in the middle of the night. Ravenous, they devoured cold chowder, soggy fried plantains and still crisp coconut shrimp before falling back into total unconsciousness.

The blast of dog breath that hit Taylor square in the face woke her the second time.

"Gawd!" Wrinkling her nose, she shagged away from the muzzle two inches from her nose. "I'm not the only one who needs a toothbrush," she muttered before twisting to look over her shoulder.

Mark was out cold beside her, his left arm bent to cover the upper half of his face. Dark bristles sprouted on the lower half.

An impatient whine drew her attention back to Tikal. His ice-blue eyes telegraphed an unmistakable message. He wanted out, or else.

"Okay, okay."

Grumbling, she eased out of bed and dressed. She had her agenda for the day fixed before she hitched up the wrinkled drawstring pants. Walk. Breakfast. Shopping.

Mark didn't stir when she left with Tikal. As the desk clerk predicted, Tropical Storm Gail had inflicted minimal damage on the hotel and its grounds. The worst Taylor and Tikal encountered were a few downed palm fronds and an overturned toolshed at the rear of the property.

Mark was awake when she returned bearing coffee, pastries and a bag of toiletries purchased at the hotel's gift shop, such as it was. His wince as he sat up to take the foam cup earned him a sympathetic cluck.

"Uh-oh. The E.R. doc said you'd feel worse before you got better."

Frowning, he probed the bandage with a tentative finger. "She was right."

"Guess we should have taken it a little easier last night."

His scowl slid into a crooked half grin. "I don't hurt that bad."

Hitching a hip on the side of the bed, Taylor fed him half of a flaky banana crisp and popped the other half in her mouth.

"You know," he said when he'd swallowed his

bite, "we should probably talk about where we want this to go."

"This being us?"

"Correct."

She chewed her bite, not really prepared for this conversation. True, they'd crossed that mythical line by trading the L-word, but some consideration could be given to the fact that they were in the crosshairs of a half dozen semiautomatic weapons at the time.

"You first," she said. "Where do you want it to go?"

He lifted a hand and wound a swatch of her hair around it. "How long will you be stationed in the D.C. area?"

"I don't know. Another year. Maybe two."

"The army's putting together a task force to study new directions in Psychological Warfare. I've been asked to consult. It would mean two to three nights a week at Fort McNair for the next six months."

"And the other nights?"

"Princeton is only three hours from D.C. We could work out a shuttle schedule."

She'd been on her own for so long. The idea of bending her life to fit around someone else's took some getting used to. Or so she thought, until she trailed a fingertip over his bristly chin.

"I'm game if you are."

A smile came into his blue eyes. "We'll make it work, Taylor. This time, we'll make it work."

"I'd suggest we seal the deal with a kiss," she said, returning the smile, "but it could lead to a repeat of last night."

He tossed her words back at her. "I'm game if you are."

She might have been sucked in if not for the wince when he lifted a hand and wrapped her nape. Giving him a quick peck, she eased out of his hold.

"We'd better seal the deal later. I talked to the desk clerk. He confirmed there wasn't much damage in town and the stores will open at nine as usual. Since I'm fairly presentable and you aren't anywhere close, I suggest you pop another couple of pills and stay put while I go into town. I'll pick up a change of clothes for both of us. Do you want jeans, slacks or dress pants?"

"Whatever's available."

"What size?"

"Thirty-four waist, thirty-three inseam."

Her glance skimmed over his bandaged chest. "Shirt?"

"Fifteen-and-a-half regular, extra large T-shirt."

"Got it. And I may try to catch Bev's insurance agent while I'm out. I want to get a rough estimate of potential damage claims against the air force before my postmission debrief with my boss."

"Think Bev will file a claim?"

"My gut says no, but you never know what'll happen when lawyers start seeing dollar signs. You rest. I'll be back in a few hours."

Mark didn't argue, which told her he hurt worse than he'd admitted. But he did drag her close for a kiss that put her paltry peck to shame.

Taylor found everything she needed at the first store she hit. Loaded down with shopping bags, she took another cab to the address Bev had given her. A hand-lettered sign stuck in the window said all agents were out assessing damage from last night's storm. The sign also gave a number to call to notify the agency of a potential claim.

Taylor jotted down the number and contemplated swinging by police headquarters for an update on Constable Benjamin's investigation and any charges that might be pending against Bev. A nagging worry about Mark nixed that idea.

He'd made a good show of it this morning but she could tell he was in more pain than he'd admitted. She had a sneaky feeling he'd go all macho and try to tough it out without the pills.

The room was empty when she let herself in. The shutters were latched back and the door to the balcony stood open. Taylor leaned on the rail, peering through the palms until she spotted Tikal lifting his leg to spray a tree trunk. Mark lounged against a brick wall close by.

They'd be up soon enough. Deciding to unwrap her purchases and display them on the bed, she went back inside.

She didn't notice the papers on the nightstand until she plunked the shopping bags on the bed. Hotel stationery, she saw with an idle glance, filled with handwritten notes.

Her gaze sharpened. The writing swam into focus. Her heart began a painful tattoo as she saw her name followed by phrases like "an excellent percipient," "rare ability to receive and project thoughts," and "mastered the portal technique in first attempt."

But it was the unfinished sentence at the bottom of the page that drove a stake through her heart. With a pain that made a mockery of the hurt she'd experienced eight years ago, she read, "Subject clearly warrants further intensive study, which I…"

She crushed the papers in her fist. Head back, eyes shut, she wrenched open the portal.

*I can't believe you did this to me!*

The cry lanced through the layers of suffocating humidity left by the storm. So anguished that Mark jerked away from the brick wall. So filled with rage that Tikal's ears went flat. Man and dog froze for a stutter of time, then turned and sprinted for the rear entrance to the hotel.

His aching chest forgotten, Mark took the stairs two at a time. Tikal lunged ahead of him. The Husky was leaping and pawing at the door to their room when Mark caught up with him. They burst in, one almost tripping over the other, and came up short at the sight of Taylor standing rigid beside the bed.

All Mark needed was one glance at the papers

bunched in her fist for understanding to hit with gale force.

"Taylor…"

"Don't!" She flung back her head, her nostrils flaring. "Don't say a word."

Her breath shuddered in, then out. Mark felt his own sit like a rock in the middle of his throat.

This was his fault for being stupid enough to leave the notes where she would find them. His mistake for not understanding how she might interpret them. His loss, he thought, his gut twisting.

As quickly as that thought had come, he shoved it aside. He'd let this woman walk away from him once. He was damned if he'd let her go again.

*Whether I walk or not depends on how you answer one question.*

His chin jerked up. "Ask it."

"Have you been putting me under a microscope all this time?"

"Yes."

She held his gaze, unblinking, unwavering. Finally her head dipped in a simple act of surrender and acceptance.

"All right. I'll be your lab rat, Mark. Whatever

I have…whatever we have together…is beyond my understanding. I accept it, but you'll have to be the one to make sense of it."

"What if I don't understand it, either?"

She unclenched her hand and smoothed the crumpled papers. "Then, as you indicate here, the subject clearly warrants further intensive study."

The tight knot in his gut loosened. She'd taken the first step. He had to take the next.

"Read that sentence in its entirety, Taylor."

"You didn't finish it."

"Yes, I did. Turn the page over and read the rest of it."

"I'm not sure I want to."

"Read it."

Blowing out a long breath, she picked up in the middle of the sentence. "…warrants further intensive study, which I…" The paper fluttered as she turned it over. "…intend to conduct over the course of the next fifty or sixty years."

She stared at the page, saying nothing more, until Mark crossed the room and took the notes from her hand. They fluttered to the floor, discarded, unneeded.

"Forty or fifty years may not be long enough."

Needing to touch her, he framed her face with his hands. "There's something about you that defies logic, defies science, defies every rational thought and leaves me with nothing but raw emotion."

The rigid set to her shoulders relaxed. He could see himself in her eyes. He saw something else as well. Something that needed no projection through time or space.

"It's called love, Wolfson."

"That's what they tell me, Chase."

\* \* \* \* \*

Look for LAST WOLF WATCHING
by Rhyannon Byrd—the exciting conclusion
in the BLOODRUNNERS miniseries
from Silhouette Nocturne.

Follow Michaela and Brody on their fierce
journey to find the truth and face the demons
from the past, as they reach the heart of the
battle between the Runners and the rogues.

Here is a sneak preview of book three,
LAST WOLF WATCHING.

Michaela squinted, struggling to see through the impenetrable darkness. Everyone looked toward the Elders, but she knew Brody Carter still watched her. Michaela could feel the power of his gaze. Its heat. Its strength. And something that felt strangely like anger, though he had no reason to have any emotion toward her. Strangers from different worlds, brought together beneath the heavy silver moon on a night made for hell itself. That was their only connection.

The second she finished that thought, she knew

it was a lie. But she couldn't deal with it now. Not tonight. Not when her whole world balanced on the edge of destruction.

Willing her backbone to keep her upright, Michaela Doucet focused on the towering blaze of a roaring bonfire that rose from the far side of the clearing, its orange flames burning with maniacal zeal against the inky black curtain of the night. Many of the Lycans had already shifted into their preternatural shapes, their fur-covered bodies standing like monstrous shadows at the edges of the forest as they waited with restless expectancy for her brother.

Her nineteen-year-old brother, Max, had been attacked by a rogue werewolf—a Lycan who preyed upon humans for food. Max had been bitten in the attack, which meant he was no longer human, but a breed of creature that existed between the two worlds of man and beast, much like the Bloodrunners themselves.

The Elders parted, and two hulking shapes emerged from the trees. In their wolf forms, the Lycans stood over seven feet tall, their legs bent at an odd angle as they stalked forward. They each held a thick chain that had been wound around their inside wrists, the twin lengths leading back into the shadows. The Lycans had taken no more than a few steps when they jerked on the chains, and her brother appeared.

Bound like an animal.

Biting at her trembling lower lip, she glanced left, then right, surprised to see that others had joined her. Now the Bloodrunners and their family and friends stood as a united force against the Silvercrest pack, which had yet to accept the fact that something sinister was eating away at its foundation—something that would rip down the protective walls that separated their world from the humans'. It occurred to Michaela that loyalties were being announced tonight—a separation made between those who would stand with the Runners in their fight against the rogues and those who blindly supported the pack's refusal to face reality. But all she could focus on was her brother. Max looked so hurt…so terrified.

"Leave him alone," she screamed, her soft-soled, black satin slip-ons struggling for purchase in the damp earth as she rushed toward Max, only to find herself lifted off the ground when a hard, heavily muscled arm clamped around her waist from behind, pulling her clear off her feet. "Damn it, let me down!" she snarled, unable to take her eyes off her brother as the golden-eyed Lycan kicked him.

Mindless with heartache and rage, Michaela clawed at the arm holding her, kicking her heels against whatever part of her captor's legs she could reach. "Stop it," a deep, husky voice grunted in her ear. "You're not helping him by losing it. I give you my word he'll survive the ceremony, but you have to keep it together."

"Nooooo!" she screamed, too hysterical to listen to reason. "You're monsters! All of you! Look what you've done to him! How dare you! *How dare you!*"

The arm tightened with a powerful flex of muscle, cinching her waist. Her breath sucked in on a sharp, wailing gasp.

"Shut up before you get both yourself and your brother killed. I will *not* let that happen. Do you understand me?" her captor growled, shaking her so hard that her teeth clicked together. "Do you understand me, Doucet?"

"Damn it," she cried, stricken as she watched one of the guards grab Max by his hair. Around them Lycans huffed and growled as they watched the spectacle, while others outright howled for the show to begin.

"That's enough!" the voice seethed in her ear. "They'll tear you apart before you even reach him, and I'll be damned if I'm going to stand here and watch you die."

Suddenly, through the haze of fear and agony and outrage in her mind, she finally recognized who'd caught her. *Brody.*

He held her in his arms, her body locked against his powerful form, her back to the burning heat of his chest. A low, keening sound of anguish tore through her, and her head dropped forward as hoarse sobs of pain ripped from her throat. "Let me go. I have to help him. *Please,*" she begged brokenly, knowing only that she needed to get to Max. "Let me go, Brody."

He muttered something against her hair, his breath warm against her scalp, and Michaela could have sworn it was a single word…. But she must have heard wrong. She was too upset. Too furious. Too terrified. She must be out of her mind.

Because it sounded as if he'd quietly snarled the word *never.*

# nocturne™

## THE FINAL INSTALLMENT OF
## THE BLOODRUNNERS TRILOGY

# Last Wolf Watching

Runner Brody Carter has found his match in
Michaela Doucet, a human with unusual psychic powers.
When Michaela's brother is threatened, Brody becomes
her protector, and suddenly not only has to protect her
from her enemies but also from himself....

## LOOK FOR
# LAST WOLF WATCHING
## BY
# RHYANNON BYRD

*Available May 2008 wherever you buy books.*

**Dramatic and Sensual Tales of Paranormal Romance**

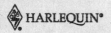
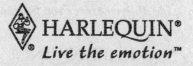

**HARLEQUIN® Romance®**

*Western Weddings*

Jason Welborn was convinced that his business partner's daughter, Jenny, had come to claim her share in the business. But Jenny seemed determined to win him over, and the more he tried to push her away, the more feisty Jenny's response. Slowly but surely she was starting to get under Jason's skin....

*Look for*

# Coming Home to the Cattleman

*by*

# JUDY CHRISTENBERRY

*Available May wherever you buy books.*

**HARLEQUIN®**
*Live the emotion™*

**www.eHarlequin.com**     HRI7511

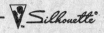

# SPECIAL EDITION™

 **THE WILDER FAMILY**
Healing Hearts in Walnut River

Social worker Isobel Suarez was proud to
work at Walnut River General Hospital, so
when Neil Kane showed up from the attorney
general's office to investigate insurance fraud,
she was up in arms. Until she melted in his
arms, and things got very tricky...

Look for

# HER MR. RIGHT?

by

## *KAREN ROSE SMITH*

*Available May wherever books are sold.*

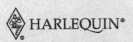

HARLEQUIN®

# *American ★ Romance*®

# Three Boys and a Baby

When Ella Garvey's eight-year-old twins and
their best friend, Dillon, discover an abandoned
baby girl, they fear she will be put in jail—
or worse! They decide to take matters into their
own hands and run away. Luckily the outlaws are
found quickly…and Ella finds a second chance
at love—with Dillon's dad, Jackson.

## LOOK FOR

# Three Boys and a Baby

## BY

# LAURA MARIE ALTOM

*Available May
wherever you buy books.*

## LOVE, HOME & HAPPINESS

# nocturne™

## COMING NEXT MONTH

**#39 LAST WOLF WATCHING • Rhyannon Byrd**
*Bloodrunners*

Brody Carter never acted on impulse—until he had to protect Michaela Doucet. A fiery psychic, the Cajun made his beast crazed, and drew his hunger. Now, as they join forces to hunt down a threat to their pack, can Brody finally let go of his own demons?

**#40 SCIONS: INSURRECTION • Patrice Michelle**
*Scions*

Investigating the mafia has NYPD detective Kaitlyn McKinney knee-deep in a supernatural war. Her only ally: Landon Rourke, a werewolf who has no love for the vampires in his city. But the secret he holds is the darkest of them all—setting everyone's tempers and passions flaring.

SNCNM0408